FOR BINNY AND NICK, IN MEMORY OF
THE MARVELOUS GAMES WE USED TO
PLAY TOGETHER AS CHILDREN

First American Edition 2016
Kane Miller, A Division of EDC Publishing

Text copyright © Kate Forsyth 2014

First published by Scholastic Press, a division of Scholastic Australia Pty Limited in 2014.
Cover illustration, maps and gifts by Jeremy Reston.
Logo design by blacksheep-uk.com.
This edition published under license from Scholastic Australia Pty Limited.
Internal photography: brick texture on pages i and iii © GiorgioMagini|istockphoto.com;
castle on page ii and folios © ivan-96|istockphoto.com; skull on page 55 © Frankie_Lee
|istockphoto.com; ring on page 73 © Czalewski|Dreamstime.com; dragon on page 84
© ZarkoCvijovic|istockphoto.com; bird on page 129 © Elena Belous|istockphoto.com;
wolf head on page 165 © Tronin Andrei|shutterstock.com.

For information contact:
Kane Miller, A Division of EDC Publishing
P.O. Box 470663
Tulsa, OK 74147-0663
www.kanemiller.com
www.edcpub.com
www.usbornebooksandmore.com

Library of Congress Control Number: 2015938785

Printed and bound in the United States of America

1 2 3 4 5 6 7 8 9 10

ISBN: 978-1-61067-414-0

KATE FORSYTH

THE IMPOSSIBLE QUEST

ESCAPE FROM WOLFHAVEN CASTLE

Kane Miller

A DIVISION OF EDC PUBLISHING

Map of Wolfhaven
& Surrounding Lands

The Witchwood

Crowthorne Castle

Rosemorran River

Blackmoor Bog

FOREST

Postern Gate

Lady's Tower

Lord's Tower

South Gatehouse

Kitchen

Well

Wolf Tower

Inner Ward

Great Hall

Outer Ward

Kennels

Stables

Garden

North Gatehouse

Well

Guards' Hall

Bell Tower

Outer Ward

Black Tower

Murder Holes

White Tower

Barbican

War Gate

TOWN

SEA

WOLFHAVEN
CASTLE

WILD MAN OF THE WOODS

"Tell your lord to beware," the wild man said, gripping Tom's arm with a dirty hand. "The wolves smell danger in the wind."

Tom tried to wrest his arm free. "What do you mean? What kind of danger?"

The wild man let go of Tom's arm, but fixed him with an intense stare from under shaggy eyebrows. He was a tall, lean man, with gray hair that hung in matted elflocks over his shoulders, and a long, tangled beard. He wore a wolf pelt and boots made of hide. His eyes were icy blue, and over one shoulder he carried a long bow and a quiver of arrows.

Tom's wolfhound, Fergus, was growling deep in

his throat, all the hairs standing up along his spine. The wild man looked down at the huge dog and said, "Quiet now."

To Tom's surprise, Fergus stopped growling, his ears pricking forward. He wagged his shaggy tail.

"Tell your lord," the wild man repeated, urgency in his voice, "danger comes." Then he turned and loped away through the forest. As he disappeared into the shadows, he flung back his head and howled like a wolf. An answering howl came from the east.

Fergus whined, straining against Tom's grip, wanting to race after the wild man. "No, Fergus, stay," Tom said. He picked up his bucket of mushrooms, dandelion leaves and nettles, which had fallen from his hand when the wild man had appeared. Tom's heart was beating hard. He had heard of the wild man of the woods, of course. People said he lived and hunted with the wolves, even in the deep snows of winter, and scorned those who huddled together behind Wolfhaven Castle's high walls. Yet Tom had never really believed the tales. He spent a lot of time in the forest, searching for rare ingredients for his mother, the castle cook. He had never seen any trace of the wild man before.

But Tom had seen him now, and felt the bruising clutch of his fingers on his arm. Rolling up his sleeve, he could see the marks where the wild man's long nails had dug in. He rubbed them, then ran down the winding path, back towards Wolfhaven Castle, his bucket swinging. Fergus bounded along beside him, ears blown back by the wind.

It took almost an hour to reach the edge of the forest. Tom paused to catch his breath. To his left, a river wound through rolling fields planted with wheat, barley, rye and old pear trees. The river led into a wide harbor protected from the wild seas by a headland and a long stone causeway. High on the cliff was a castle with six round towers, crowned with pointed roofs.

With his dog at his heels, Tom crossed the humped bridge with its five stone arches and walked along the road into the town. As always the narrow, cobbled streets were crowded with people and Tom had to push his way through. He dragged Fergus away from the enticing smells of the marketplace, where fishmongers, butchers and bakers shouted their wares.

It was a steep climb up the main street, and Tom was short of breath by the time he reached the arched castle gate at the top of the road. Tall and wide enough to let through a band of giants, the iron-barred gate was secured fast. Tom had never seen the gate open, for it was only unlocked in times of war. A much smaller door had been cut into the base of the gate, to let the castle folk in and out. Two men stood guard, leaning on their spears.

"Afternoon, Tom," the guard named Morgan said, and opened the door to let him through.

"Do you know anything about the wild man of the woods?" Tom asked.

"Why?" Morgan asked. "You seen him?"

Tom nodded. "He grabbed me in the forest. Told me to tell my lord that danger comes."

Morgan frowned. "Danger?" He scanned the landscape, drowsy and serene under the hot summer sun, then shrugged. "No danger that I can see."

"He said the wolves smelled danger in the wind."

"Crazy loon," the other guard, Gareth, said.

"I wouldn't worry," Morgan said. "Gareth's right, the wild man's as mad as a March hare. Must be, to live out there in the wilderness instead of staying safe inside the castle walls."

"I must tell the master-of-arms, just in case," Tom said.

Gareth sniggered. "Good luck with that, son."

"He'll laugh his socks off," added Morgan. "Then give you a clip over the ear for wasting his time."

Both guards laughed. Tom felt his face grow hot. With Fergus beside him, he went through the door and into the courtyard of the barbican, surrounded by high stone walls set with window slits. Murder holes, they were called. Anyone who managed to break through the war gate would be shot down, or have boiling oil poured on their heads, before they got any deeper into the castle.

Tom went through a long passage into the castle's inner ward. To the left was the long building that housed the kitchen and storerooms that were his mother's domain. To the right was the guardhouse, with an archway that led through to the jousting yard. Ahead was the garden, with the great bulk of the castle behind, built of honey-colored stone that glowed in the afternoon sun.

Tom stood for a moment outside the guardroom, hesitating. Remembering the urgency in the wild man's voice, Tom took a deep breath and went inside.

"Can I see the master-of-arms?" Tom asked, taking off his shabby blue hat.

"What for?" the guard said, looking up from polishing his boots.

"I need to get a message to my lord. The wild man of the woods says to beware, there's danger coming."

The guard laughed. "Scram, boy," he said. "Sir Kevyn is busy getting ready for the mob-ball match this afternoon. He has no time for stories."

"But what if the wild man knows something we don't?"

But the soldier just flapped a hand at him to go away, and went back to polishing his boots.

Tom crammed his hat back on his head and stepped outside. He could hear yells and grunts coming from the jousting yard, and headed that way.

Rows of brawny squires were charging as fast as they could towards thick leather bolsters held upright by other boys.

Thwack, went their shoulders into the bolsters.

Smack, went the boys, down into the dust.

Ooof, they gasped.

Hooray, shouted those still standing.

Tom watched enviously. He loved mob-ball, but he was kept too busy in the kitchen to ever get much of a chance to play.

Sir Kevyn, the master-of-arms, shouted, "Bring 'em down! You call that running? Come on, run! Run, I say! Knock 'em down!"

He was a burly man in polished chain metal, with a nose that looked as if it had been broken a great many times. His fists were enormous. He shook them as he shouted, "Run! If you're not prepared to hurt 'em, you shouldn't be in the game!"

At last he noticed Tom.

"What is it, boy? What do you want?" he bellowed.

All the squires stopped and turned to stare at Tom.

Tom stumbled through his message, which sounded

more stupid with each retelling. The master-of-arms stared at him, astounded, then put his fists on his hips and roared with laughter. All the squires copied him, laughing and pointing at Tom.

"Ooooh, the wolves smell danger," mocked a tall boy with unruly red hair.

"Is this some kind of midsummer foolery?" the master-of-arms asked, when at last he caught his breath.

"No, sir. He told me I had to warn the lord . . ." Tom answered.

"As if a scrawny little pot boy like you would ever get to speak to Lord Wolfgang," the redhead said.

The master-of-arms scowled at him. "Did I give you permission to speak, Lord Sebastian?"

"No, sir!"

"Did I say you were allowed to stop running?"

"No, sir!"

"Then run, you thickhead!"

"Yes, sir!" Sebastian at once charged down the field, giving Tom a furious glance as he did so.

The master-of-arms looked back at Tom, arms

crossed. "Go on, get out of here. You think I've time for such hogwash?"

"No, sir," Tom said, and trudged away, Fergus at his heels. As he passed the squires, he heard Sebastian call out, "Back to the kitchen where you belong, pot boy!"

MISTRESS ⟶ PIPPIN

"Stir the soup!" the castle cook shouted. "Grease the goose! Peel the eels! Pummel the pastry! Are those blackbirds ready for the pie?"

She was a small, plump woman, with rosy cheeks and fair hair pinned up under a white cap. The pockets of her long white apron bristled with wooden spoons, soup ladles and basting brushes, and a huge key ring jangled at her belt.

As she called out commands, people rushed to do her bidding.

A woman carrying a tall, wobbling jelly in the shape of the castle, almost collided with a man with a barrel of eels on his shoulder. Another man hurried in with a stick hung with pheasants, while girls in white aprons and caps stood in a row at the long table, knives flashing as they chopped leeks at high speed.

It was boiling hot. Everyone's face was red and damp. Fires blazed at either hearth, and as the bakers opened the bread ovens and slid the bread pans in and out, hot air lifted in clouds of wavering heat. Beside each fire, a small dog ran around and around in a wheel, turning the great haunches of wild boar on their spits, fat sputtering as it splashed onto the coals. One woman was plucking blackbirds in a storm of dark feathers. Another was breaking eggs into a bowl and whisking them into a yellow froth. Yet another was grinding herbs and oil in a granite mortar.

The cook now stood at a huge cauldron hung above one of the fires. A thin man hurried to bring her a stool. She hopped up onto it nimbly, and bent to sniff the soup. The thin man—who was twice as tall as the cook—twisted his hands together. The cook frowned and drew out a long-handled spoon from her apron. She scooped up a tiny spoonful of broth and sipped it. Her frown deepened. The thin man gnawed his fingernails, while everyone nearby turned to watch, holding their breath in anticipation.

"Perhaps some thyme," the cook said, and the thin man rushed to get her a sprig of the sweet-scented herb. She stripped off the leaves and dropped them one by one into the soup, sniffing the steam that roiled out of the cauldron. "Mmmm. Maybe a smidgen of salt."

"Yes, Mistress Pippin, of course. More salt," he said. He grabbed a bowl of sea salt crystals, and the cook took a tiny pinch and sprinkled it into the soup. She stirred it once, twice, thrice, then plucked a fresh spoon from her apron and took another tiny sip. Slowly she nodded her head. "Perfect."

The thin man beamed in delight, and everyone around him shook his hand and congratulated him. The cook jumped down from her stool, and smoothed her apron. Then Tom's stomach rumbled loudly. It had been a long time since breakfast, and the steam from the soup smelled delicious.

The cook turned around, hands on hips. "Tom, at last! Where have you been all this time? Did you find my mushrooms?"

"Yes . . ." Tom began. He badly wanted to tell his mother about the wild man's warning, but she did not give him a chance.

"My nettles?"

"Yes."

"My dandelion leaves?"

"Yes, Mam."

"Well, what are you waiting for?" Tom's mother seized the bucket from him and emptied it on the table. "Maude, begin the mushroom and quail pasties!" She scooped up all the mushrooms into a bowl and threw it across the table to another white-capped woman, who squeaked and just managed to catch it. "Nancy, get to work on the nettle soup." Tom's mother tossed the bunch of stinging nettles across the room to a girl who caught it, then cried "Ow!" and promptly dropped the bunch on the floor. "Sorry, Mistress Pippin." She scooped up the nettles, tossed them from hand to hand, then threw them into the nearby sink to wash.

Tom's mother seized a knife and began to chop up the dandelion leaves so fast her knife was a mere blur.

At once all the other women began to chop faster too. The thunk of metal against wood echoed among the beams.

"Right, Tom, I need you to get started on all those pots," said Mistress Pippin as she chopped, "and then you can help the footmen polish the silver. We have unexpected guests for the midsummer feast tonight, and need to lay another two dozen places . . . and get that dog out of my butter barrel!"

Tom dragged Fergus's nose away from the butter, wondering how his mother had known what the wolfhound was doing. "Mam," he said, but she was too busy chopping to hear him. He called her again, more loudly this time, and his mother paused and looked at him in surprise. "What is it, Tomkin?"

"I . . . I met the wild man in the woods today."

Mistress Pippin's knife fell with a clatter to the floor. She stared at Tom, eyes round. "The wild man?"

When Tom nodded, she looked around her, as if making sure nobody was watching or listening, then caught Tom's shoulder and drew him down the kitchen and into the chill of the buttery. Once she had shut

ESCAPE FROM WOLFHAVEN CASTLE

─────────────┤ 1 ├─────────────

the door behind them, she said urgently, "What did
he say, Tom?"

He told her, and somehow, the words no longer
seemed stupid, but as charged with danger and
meaning as when the wild man had spoken them in
the shadowy tangle of the forest.

"He said I have to tell the lord, but . . . Mam, no
one will listen to me."

"Of course you must tell the lord," she said. She
took Tom's hand and marched him out of the buttery,
through the kitchen, and up the stairs to the butler's
pantry, Fergus trotting behind.

"Tom has important news," she told the butler. "I
tell you, he must see the lord."

"See the lord? Young Tom? Not likely," the butler
answered.

"You make sure he sees the lord, or there'll be no
more spiced pear and butterscotch pudding for you,"
Mistress Pippin warned.

The butler sat up at once, almost popping all
his buttons in his haste. "No need for that, Mistress
Pippin, I'll do what I can!"

She left Tom there, and raced back to her kitchen so fast the ribbons of her cap streamed behind her.

Tom told his tale again. The butler hummed and hawed, but took Tom to the castle steward.

Tom told his tale yet again. The steward rasped his chin and frowned, but took Tom to see the chamberlain.

Tom told the tale one more time, feeling like an absolute fool. The chamberlain yawned and stretched, then mumbled that he would pass the message on, if he could just find the time. He waved Tom away, then lay back in his chair, spread his handkerchief over his face, and promptly began to snore.

By that time, Tom was so frustrated that he felt as if steam was about to burst out of his ears. He stood for a moment, wondering if he dared go up the stairs to the great hall and accost Lord Wolfgang himself. Tom was fairly sure the lord's bodyguards would simply kick him back down again. So, scowling, he went down the stairs, wondering what else he could do.

A girl, dressed in white with bare feet and a wild mass of curly black hair, was sitting in a window archway, studying an enormous book. She looked up as he slouched by, and raised her eyebrows. "You know that there are only three words that end in the sound 'gree'? You look like two of them, at least."

"I'm not in the mood for riddles, Quinn," Tom snapped.

"Of course not, since riddles are for the wise," she answered, her turquoise green eyes gleaming. "Still, I'm sure you'll a*gree*, you're an*gry* and hun*gry*, so riddle me ree, can you tell me all three?"

"Go boil your head," Tom replied and jumped down two steps at once to get past her. Quinn had become a lot more annoying since she had been apprenticed to the castle witch, he thought.

"You go boil yours," she answered and stuck out her tongue at him.

3

»———→ MOB-BALL ←———«

A huge roar from the jousting yard rang through the inner ward.

The mob-ball game must have started.

Tom had no wish to scrub pots, and so he hurried away from the kitchen and ran instead towards the playing fields. Fergus bounded beside him, his tail wagging.

The stands were filled with crowds of people, shouting and waving flags and drinking pear cider, called "merrylegs" by some, and "mumblehead" by others, for its effect on those who drank it. In the center of the field, boys in green or red jerkins jostled and fought over the ball, which was made from an inflated pig's bladder.

Tom had watched the game many times, and knew the squires in red always beat the serving boys. They had time to train and play against each other, while the serving boys were always too busy with their work to have much free time to practice.

One serving boy in green seized the ball and ran towards the goalposts at the far end of the yard, but the redheaded squire, Sebastian, put out one foot to trip him, and he fell flat on his face. Sebastian grabbed the ball and ran towards the other end. Three boys in green caught him around the waist and shoulders, but Sebastian just kept on running, dragging them along behind him. One by one they fell, and were trampled under the rush of feet as everyone raced after the redheaded boy. One of the boys came up howling, both hands clamped across a bloody nose, and he was pulled off the field by a man-at-arms, his head dunked into a bucket of icy water. There were no rules in mob-ball, only speed, strength, and bravado.

On impulse, Tom ran up to the boy with the bloody nose. "Your team's one man down now. Give me your jerkin."

The boy with the bleeding nose pulled off his green jerkin. "Watch out," he warned. "The squires play rough."

Tom nodded, shrugging himself into the jerkin. He and his friends played mob-ball together whenever they could, but Tom had never played in an official midsummer match before. His time spent roaming the forest had made him lean and swift, and his arms were strong from scrubbing pots. He was sure he could hold his own against those rough squires.

He ran out into the field, just as Sebastian kicked the ball towards the goalposts. Tom jumped high, caught the ball, and began to run towards the far end of the field. It felt good to be in motion, and even better to be playing against those arrogant young lords who had mocked him earlier. Tom was determined to show that he was just as good as they were, even if he was just a lowly pot boy. He dodged and swerved, slipping through the hands that reached to yank him down. Fergus ran with him, barking with joy.

"Get him!" Sebastian shouted, as he launched himself at Tom's back. Tom sidestepped, and Sebastian hit the dirt. The castle servants all roared with laughter, cheering and shaking their green flags. Sebastian got up, scowling, covered in dust. Tom sidestepped another red-clad squire, then kicked a goal. The ball soared high and went straight through the posts. All the serving boys cheered and slapped Tom on the back.

Sebastian glowered at Tom. "You'd better watch out," he muttered, and launched himself at Tom as soon as the whistle blew.

Tom seized the ball and ran with it. He felt Sebastian's hands close on his jerkin, but the material tore in half, and Tom leapt free. Once again Sebastian ended up facedown in the dirt. Tom fell down too, grazing his knee, but he scrambled up and ran on. He could hear Sebastian's heavy footsteps pounding behind him, so put on a burst of speed. It was as if all his anger and frustration gave his feet wings. He ran all the way to the other end of the field, and dived through the goalposts to score another goal.

Fergus barked and leapt up to lick Tom's face. Then the rest of his teammates reached him, shouting in delight.

"It's two-all now," a stable boy cried. "We just need one more goal and we'll beat the squires for the first time in seventeen years!"

The whistle blew, and Sebastian kicked the ball hard. It practically flew the whole length of the field. Tom ran as fast as he could, determined not to let him score another goal. Sebastian was running too, but Tom was faster. He got to the ball a scant second before the squire, and kicked it away. The gardener's boy caught it and ran like a hare. He passed it to a stable boy, who passed it to a pot boy, who passed it to the falconer's apprentice, who passed it to Tom.

Then Sebastian took him down. As Tom hit the dirt, the ball flew up out of his hands. Sebastian jumped for it, but Fergus leapt past him, snatching the ball in his jaws. The wolfhound landed lightly on all four paws, and began to snarl and shake the ball as if it was a rat. One boy after another tried to seize it from him, but the dog would not let go.

"That's not fair! A dog can't play!" Sebastian cried.

"No rules in mob-ball," Tom panted, racing up to Fergus. "Drop it, boy."

Fergus dropped it obediently. Tom grabbed the ball and ran for the goal line.

Feet pounded behind him. He feinted, sidestepped, and swerved unexpectedly to the left. Sebastian hurtled past him and landed flat in the dust again.

Tom kicked the ball as hard as he could, and it soared between the goals. Tom cheered and raised his arms in victory, running back towards his new teammates who hoisted him high on their shoulders. Green flags waved wildly. All the servants cheered and whistled and crashed together their tankards of pear cider.

"Flat-footed fools!" the master-of-arms bellowed at the crestfallen squires. "You'll be up at dawn and training till midnight from now on, you thick-heads!"

As Tom was carried from the field, high on the shoulders of his teammates, he looked back at Sebastian, getting up from the dirt where he had been well and truly trampled. "I'm going to get you," the squire mouthed at him. "Just you wait."

Later that afternoon, Tom trudged up from the cellar, carrying a heavy wicker-wrapped bottle of mead, made with honey from the castle's own bees. He walked slowly, his body aching from the mob-ball game, his thoughts once more occupied with the wild man's warning and his failure to deliver it. Why would no one listen to him? What if the castle really was in danger?

Fergus growled deep in his throat, and Tom at once tensed. He heard a soft shuffle of feet around the corner. He went back down a few steps and pressed against the stone wall.

Then Sebastian leapt out at him.

Tom hit him over the head with the wicker bottle. As Sebastian fell, Tom leapt over him and raced up the stairs. Fergus bounded after him.

"I'll get you!" Sebastian shouted.

Tom ran past the kitchen doorway and plunged through a tapestry-hung archway. It led to the servants' stairs, a steep, narrow set that curled inside the walls of the castle so servants did not have to carry chamber pots or trays of dirty dishes where the lords and ladies might see them. Tom had hoped Sebastian would not see him duck through the tapestry curtain, but he wasn't quick enough. In seconds, the redheaded squire was after him again. With Fergus bounding ahead, Tom leapt up the steps as fast as he could.

The staircase branched, the left-hand turn leading to a staircase that spiraled up into the Lady's Tower. Tom scrambled that way, bent over double and using his hands to get along faster. Then Fergus ran straight under the feet of a servant carrying a tray. The servant fell head over heels down the stairs, wiping out Sebastian as he fell. *Clang, clatter, clank, crash,* the two of them tumbled all the way down to the bottom.

Tom kept clambering upward, taking one turn, then another, till he was climbing higher into the castle than he'd ever been before. It looked like no one had been there in centuries. Dust lay thick on the steps. Cobwebs hung in filthy tatters. Bats screeched away into the shadows.

Fergus whined. His ears and tail drooped.

"Now we just need to find a way out," Tom said, searching for a window or door in the walls that would give him some sense of where he was. "One that doesn't involve going back the way we came."

His feet stirred up clouds of dust. Fergus sneezed.

They kept on climbing. The staircase had become so narrow that Tom's shoulders brushed against the wall on either side, while the steps were so steep that it was like climbing a cliff. His calf muscles ached, and his throat was dry. "Maybe we should go back," Tom murmured, slowing.

Fergus whined and ran forward eagerly, pushing his nose against a faded old tapestry. He looked back at Tom and whined again.

"What have you found, boy?" Tom asked.

The tapestry showed a maiden sitting in a meadow, a dark unicorn lying with its head resting in her lap. As Tom lifted it aside, the fabric crumbled away in his hand and revealed a tiny door.

He bent and examined the cobwebby key perched in the lock. He tried to turn it, but it was so stiff, it wouldn't budge. He persisted, and the key finally turned with a nerve-shredding screech. Fergus whined and pressed close to Tom. Tom pushed at the door. It wouldn't open.

He pushed harder.

Suddenly it swung open. Tom fell through with a crash, Fergus landing right on top of him.

4

A LADY'S COMPLETE GUIDE TO
MANNERS, MORALS
« & MODESTY »

L ady Elanor stared drearily at the wall.

She wished her governess, Mistress Mauldred, would at least put her by the window so she had something to look at while she was strapped in her backboard. She wished Mistress Mauldred had chosen a lighter book than *A Lady's Complete Guide to Manners, Morals & Modesty* to balance on top of her head. She wished Mistress Mauldred would come back and unstrap her.

Suddenly there was a terrible screeching noise. Elanor looked slowly towards the sound, careful not to make the book topple off her head.

A section of the oak paneling in her room flung

open and a boy and a dog came crashing through onto the floor.

The boy was very dirty.

The dog was very large and very hairy.

Elanor stared in astonishment.

The boy sat up, rubbing his head. His dusty blond hair fell into his eyes, which were as blue as the vase of forget-me-nots on Elanor's table. "Get off me," he said, pushing the dog away. The dog licked him lovingly. "Must you always lick me?" the boy complained. "You have the wettest tongue in the world." He looked up and saw Elanor.

She stared at him.

He stared back. "Who are you?" he asked.

"I am Lady Elanor Morwenna Grace de Belleterre, daughter of Wolfgang de Belleterre, Lord of Wolfhaven Castle." She smoothed her green silk dress over her knees.

"Fungus!" Tom exclaimed, then went red. "Sorry. I shouldn't . . ."

"I don't mind," Elanor said quickly. "So who are you?"

"I'm Tom Pippin. The cook's son."

"What are you doing here?"

"Someone was chasing me."

"Why?"

He shrugged. "It doesn't really matter. I'm sorry to crash in on you. I didn't know where I was."

"No matter," she said.

"Why do you have a book stuck on your head?"

"*A lady must always hold her head high*," Elanor replied.

"And why are you strapped up to that thing?"

"*A lady must not slump*."

"Do you want to be strapped up like that?"

"Not in the least."

"Would you like me to unstrap you?"

"If you would be so kind."

Tom unstrapped her and took the thick, heavy book off her head, tossing it onto a chair. Elanor rubbed her sore neck.

"Have you been strapped up for long?"

"It feels like half the day," she answered. "Thank you for releasing me."

"No problem," he replied, looking around the room.

Elanor wondered what he thought of it. By the way his eyes widened with amazement, she guessed he was not used to such a grand room. Hung with velvet curtains the color of lilacs, her bed was set up on a stage, and was big enough for twenty. Her chair was upholstered in lilac velvet too, and was big enough for five.

The boy's eyes stopped upon her tea tray, set on the table near the fireplace. His mouth fell open.

"Are you hungry?" she asked.

"Starving," he replied.

"Would you care to join me for tea?"

"Would I?" he cried, then hesitated. "What if someone comes in?" he asked.

"No one will," she answered. "And if they do, you can escape out that secret door again." She regarded the doorway with thoughtful eyes, and decided it was best not to mention it to Mistress Mauldred. "Would you mind shutting it? For now?"

As Tom shut the secret door, Elanor piled a plate with cucumber and borage sandwiches, tiny scones with damson plum jam and cream, slivers of cold ham, and a roasted quail leg, encrusted with salt and thyme, then passed the laden plate to Tom.

Tom dropped in his chair, seized his plate, and ate enthusiastically. Fergus sat by his side, his shaggy head level with Tom's shoulder, and fixed him with imploring eyes. Tom tossed him some ham, which he snatched and swallowed in a single gulp. Elanor filled her own plate, then put the platter of ham down on the floor for Fergus. With a gulp and a guzzle, the wolfhound cleared it in seconds.

"Manners, Fergus," Tom said automatically, then removed his elbows from the table.

Elanor smiled. "Eat up," she said. "I'm very hungry too."

Tom was puzzling something over. "Did you have to sit there, all strapped up to that thing, with your tea sitting right in front of you?"

Elanor nodded. "*Ladies must learn self-restraint.*"

"That's awful," Tom said.

"*Ladies must learn not to be greedy.*"

"Who strapped you up like that, and left you to stare at your tea?"

"My governess, Mistress Mauldred," Elanor answered. "A most estimable lady," she added, after a moment.

They ate in comfortable silence, Fergus begging from first one, then the other. This made Elanor feel happy. She had always wanted a dog of her own, but Mistress Mauldred said that dogs were too rough, noisy and smelly. It was true the wolfhound was rather malodorous, but he took the food from Elanor's fingers with great delicacy and, when she ruffled his ears, they were as soft as velvet.

"I never knew there was a door in my paneling," Elanor said, dabbing her mouth with her napkin. "I'm not sure if I'm glad or frightened. I mean, it's nice to know I could go down to the stables and go for a ride without Mistress Mauldred knowing. However, I'm not sure I like knowing someone could creep into my room at any time of day or night."

"There was a key in the door. You could lock it from your side and then unlock it anytime you please," Tom said.

Elanor smiled. She made a plan there and then to

go down and visit her pony that very afternoon. She would go for a ride by the seashore and gallop along the edge of the waves. Mistress Mauldred always said ladies must not trot, or canter, or indeed go any faster than the slowest amble, but Elanor loved to gallop. Her mother had always let her ride as fast as she liked, when she was alive.

A hammering came from the other side of the secret door. Elanor stood up, her throat closing over. Tom dived behind the bed, then reached out a long arm, grabbed Fergus by his ruff, and dragged him into hiding too.

"Who's there?" Elanor quavered.

The secret door swung open, and a very grubby boy with flame-colored curls tumbled face-first onto her carpet. She recognized him at once. He was Lord Sebastian Byrne, son of one of the country's most powerful nobles, Lord Aiden of Ashbyrne Castle. Sebastian had come to live at Wolfhaven Castle a few months earlier, as a squire in training to be a knight.

Elanor straightened her back and said as coldly as she could, "Who are you? How dare you invade my

ESCAPE FROM WOLFHAVEN CASTLE

private quarters?" (*Ladies must always command respect,*
she had always been told.)

"My lady!" Sebastian scrambled to his feet and
bowed deeply, almost overbalancing. "My apologies. I
was pursuing a disorderly knave . . . I thought he came
this way."

"You expect to find a knave in my private quarters?"
(*Ladies must be dignified at all times.*)

"No, no, of course not . . . it's just I saw his footsteps
in the dust . . ."

"You do seem to have been rolling around in a
great deal of filth," Elanor replied, putting her nose
in the air.

The redhead looked down at himself, then tried to
brush the dust away. Great clouds rose all around him.

"I'm sorry," he managed to splutter, his tawny-
colored eyes watering. "Obviously I was mistaken."

"Obviously." (*Ladies never disagree with a gentleman.*)

"I'll just go . . . beg pardon, my lady . . . sorry for
all the cobwebs . . ." Bowing low again and again, the
boy backed out through the secret door. Elanor shut
it after him, locked it, and put the key in her pocket.

She felt giddy with excitement.

"You were great," Tom said, crawling out from behind the bed. "Did you see how low he bowed? His nose practically scraped the floor."

Fergus bounded out, tail wagging, sending the dust swirling high again. Both Tom and Elanor sneezed and wheezed.

"I shall be in terrible trouble when my governess returns," Elanor said, when she could catch her breath. "Look how grimy my room is!"

"I'll help you tidy up. If there's one thing I'm good at, it's cleaning." Tom took up the rug and shook it out the window, banged the cushions together, then mopped the dust off the furniture with his napkin. "I'll take the tray away for you. Then your governess need never know you ate it all."

"I can tell her quite truthfully that a servant cleared it away," Elanor said.

Tom began to pack up the tray. "My lady," he began, rather hesitantly, wanting to tell Lady Elanor about the wild man's warning. "I've been trying all day to get a message to your father, but . . . everyone's too busy or too . . . anyway, if I tell it to you, will you let your father know?"

"Oh, I . . ." Elanor hesitated. "The Lord of Frostwick Castle is here most unexpectedly, to talk of trade and . . . and such things. Father will be busy." (*Ladies never interrupt their elders.*)

"I really do think it's important," Tom answered.

Elanor bit her lip, then smiled shyly. "I could try, I suppose."

MIDSUMMER FEAST

Sebastian was bruised all over. In body and in spirit. What would his father say if he knew his son had let a mere pot boy beat him at mob-ball, knock him down the stairs, and then led him tumbling into a young lady's chamber?

His father would not be pleased.

Trumpets blew. Sebastian straightened his aching back. The doors were flung open, and Lord Wolfgang and his daughter entered the room. They were both dressed in green, Lady Elanor wearing a silk dress with dangling sleeves embroidered with gold thread to match her golden slippers. The lord had once been a tall man, but now his shoulders stooped, his beard was more silver than fair, and his face was lined with weariness. Lord Wolfgang had not been the same since his wife had died, Sebastian's mother said. He spent all his time alone in his study, and hardly seemed to notice he had a daughter who was the spitting image of her mother. Sebastian found that hard to believe. Lord Wolfgang's wife, Morwenna, had been beautiful, judging by her portrait on the wall. Lady Elanor just seemed skinny and anxious, with hazel eyes that were too big for her face. "Father, please listen to me," she was saying as they came to their chairs.

"Now don't you worry your pretty head about a thing," he told her, looking as if his thoughts were elsewhere.

"Please, Father, if you'd just listen . . ."

"Lady Elanor," her governess said, "how many times must I tell you that ladies simply do not speak unless spoken to? Your father is a busy man; he has no time for your nonsense."

"But, Mistress Maul—"

"Ladies do not begin a sentence with 'but,'" her governess interrupted.

"I'm sorry, Mistress Mauldred, it is just . . ."

"Lady Elanor! Ladies never interrupt. Sit down, back straight, elbows by your side, hands folded in your lap, and do not speak again unless spoken to."

Lady Elanor's shoulders slumped.

"Lady Elanor! Ladies never slouch!"

Lady Elanor sat as straight as if someone had tied a poker to her spine. Sebastian couldn't help feeling sorry for her.

After the lord and his daughter, came a procession of nobles clad in midsummer finery. Arwen, the Grand Teller, came in, a tall staff in one hand. As always, Arwen was dressed in a simple white robe, her silvery hair waving down her back. Her back was straight, although her skin was like old parchment. Her only ornament was a wooden talisman hung on a thong around her neck. It was carved into an old man's face, with oak leaves instead of hair.

Behind Arwen walked her apprentice, a thin girl with wild black hair and turquoise green eyes. Both witch and apprentice were barefoot, with wreaths of golden flowers on their heads and a black-handled knife hanging from their belts. Sebastian stared at the witch girl hard. He'd heard that she had been found as a baby in a basket, bobbing up and down on the waves. It did not seem at all respectable.

The witch girl felt his gaze and scowled at him. Sebastian went red.

After the nobles came the rest of the castle folk, from the chamberlain all the way down to the humblest laundry maid. They sat at long tables that lined the great hall, with wooden platters and cups instead of silver plates and goblets. Sebastian kept a close eye out for the pot boy, and saw him come in towards the end, his huge shaggy dog at his heels as always. Sebastian glowered at him, and the pot boy grinned at him mockingly. Sebastian could only endure it in silence. Sadly, a squire was not permitted to start a fight during a feast.

When everyone was seated, the trumpets sounded again and a small party of grand strangers swept in. They were greeted by the steward and shown to chairs at the high table.

Lord Wolfgang stood. "Lord Mortlake, welcome to

Wolfhaven Castle. We hope you have a pleasant stay with us, and enjoy our feast."

The leader of the strangers inclined his iron-gray head and smiled. He was a handsome man, with dark eyes and an eagle nose. Sebastian stared at him with interest, knowing he was the Lord of Frostwick Castle, in the cold, mountainous lands to the north. Sebastian's mother always said they bred them tough up there, and indeed Lord Mortlake seemed strong and stern.

The witch stood up, and the room fell silent. She raised high her silver goblet. "Merry midsummer to you all!" she cried.

Everyone cheered and clashed their cups and goblets together. Then the feast began. Sebastian was not permitted to eat until all the nobles at the high table had finished, and so he rushed to carve the roast boar, and pour goblets of mead.

Lord Wolfgang and Lord Mortlake were discussing trade routes. Mistress Mauldred was instructing Lady Elanor how to eat her food like a lady. Elanor looked as if she had something to say to her father but had no idea how to interrupt him.

Sebastian wished he could sit down at the servants' table, where everyone was singing and laughing and eating with gusto, tossing tidbits to the dogs under the tables. They looked like they were having fun. Except for the pot boy, who was most inappropriately making faces at Lady Elanor, as if urging her to do something. Sebastian frowned at him, but then Lord Mortlake clicked his fingers for more mead, and Sebastian hurried forward with the bottle.

"I'm sorry, my daughter is far too young to be thinking of marriage," Lord Wolfgang said. "Besides, I hope that she will, in time, marry for love, as I did."

"Of course," Lord Mortlake said, though he looked as if something disgusting had been shoved under his nose. "But my dear son Cedric is already quite taken with your pretty daughter, and I'm sure she shall find him most pleasant company."

The dear son Cedric was shoveling food into his mouth as fast as he could, splashing gravy all over his shirt. It was a mystery where he put it all, for he was the skinniest kid Sebastian had ever seen. Lord Mortlake elbowed his son, and Cedric looked up. "What?" he said, his mouth full of roast boar.

"Weren't you saying before how very pretty you think Lady Elanor is?" his father prompted.

Cedric looked aghast. He glanced at Elanor, who sat bolt upright, her brow knotted with anxiety. "Err . . . umm . . . yes. Very . . . umm . . . nice."

"Perhaps after dinner you two could walk in the garden together," Lord Mortlake said.

"My daughter is only twelve," Lord Wolfgang said. "Far too young to be thinking about such things. Besides, they are kin. Such talk is unseemly!"

"They don't need to be married now," Lord Mortlake said. "But it's always wise to plan for the future, don't you agree, my dear Lord Wolfgang? Let's take the dowry into account. Your daughter is, of course, more priceless than rubies. But we would be happy to settle for the rights to use the river and the harbor."

"We have spoken about this before," Lord Wolfgang said. "My father revoked your father's rights to use the Wolfhaven River because he refused to pay the tolls and taxes. Then your father burned down the harbormaster's house and half the town."

"Ah, ancient history," Lord Mortlake said, waving his pheasant leg. The huge ring on his right hand flashed red. "Let bygones be bygones."

"Well, then, what of the issue of piracy?" Lord Wolfgang said. "Men from your land keep raiding our riverboats and stealing all our cargo."

"No! Really? I fear you must be mistaken, my lord. Thieves and bandits are everywhere, I admit, but I am sure those river pirates you speak of do not come from my land. We have no river, remember."

"I'm afraid I will not discuss the matter of rights to use *my* river until I've been compensated for all *my* losses," Lord Wolfgang said. "And I certainly will not discuss my daughter's marriage! Not for another ten years!"

Elanor smiled gratefully at her father, but Lord Wolfgang did not notice.

Lord Mortlake grimaced and crushed a walnut shell to powder in his hand.

The servants cleared away the platters of gnawed

bones and brought out jellies and meringues and crystallized violets. More mead was poured at the high table, while another barrel of pear cider was rolled out for the lower tables.

When everyone's lips and fingers were shiny with sugar, the Grand Teller rose and went to stand before the fireplace at the head of the hall. Its carved stone mantel arched far above her head, displaying two massive keys crossed one over the other. Sebastian knew that they were the keys to the war gate, only opened when the castle was under attack. One key was black and the other white, and both were longer and thicker than his arm.

"It is time for the midsummer tale," Arwen said. A murmur of anticipation rose, and she waited till all was quiet again.

"Long, long ago, enemies came over the waves to Wolfhaven Castle, with lightning in their hands and darkness in their souls. The people of the land were filled with terror. It seemed as if all must die. Four great heroes arose, seizing weapons made of flame and wind and stone and sea . . ."

Sebastian forgot how hungry and tired and sore he was, and listened, enraptured. That witch sure knew how to tell a good story. The story was filled with perilous quests and mighty battles and fearsome beasts. At times the Grand Teller's whole body changed, growing and swaying as if she herself was a snake, or shrinking and crouching as if she was a tiny mouse, her voice nothing but a frightened squeak. Once she flung her arms wide, and for an instant the shadows of huge wings wavered over the stone walls.

"Back to back, the heroes stood, fighting with the last strength left in their arms." Arwen thrust and feinted with an imaginary sword, her face set as hard as any warrior facing death. "But as they hacked and hewed at the mighty beast, the spatters of its shattered body rose up into fearsome life again, a dozen, ten dozen, a hundred, a thousand, ten thousand more . . ." Arwen's voice quickened and grew shrill. She raised her arms. Sebastian forgot to breathe.

The Grand Teller did not speak for a long moment. Her hands dropped. The great hall was utterly silent. Arwen leaned forward. Very quietly, she said, "Then, with a mighty roar, the dragon at last answered the call and swooped through the cavern, his flaming breath blasting that multitude of ravenous beasts into nothing more than a swirl of ashes and smoke."

Her hands circled, her arms snaking out. The candle flames guttered, smoke eddying through the air.

"Our heroes fell to their knees. They laughed. They wept. And so the land was saved."

A great sigh rose from the audience.

Arwen dropped her hands from her face and looked around the great hall. "They say the four heroes still sleep, somewhere under our very feet, in the hollow mountain beneath the castle. One day, when Wolfhaven Castle has need of them, they shall wake and fight to save us once more.

"By bone, over stone, through flame, out of ice, with breath, to banish death," she intoned. "One day the sleeping warriors will arise again."

Then she folded her hands and bowed her head low. Applause echoed around the hall. People sitting at the lower tables stamped their feet and banged their tankards together. Sebastian quickly gathered himself and hurried to fill the goblets of the lord and guests so they too could drink a toast to the witch. He noticed that Tom was staring at Lady Elanor again, grimacing and jerking his head to one side. Lady Elanor looked anxious. Sebastian felt his ears turn hot and red. That pot boy needed a lesson in how to behave respectfully towards his betters!

Lord Mortlake did not drink, but only clenched his hand around his goblet as if trying to crush that to powder too. When at last the applause died down, he rose to his feet and clapped his hands sharply.

Silence fell. Everyone turned to stare at him. He showed his teeth in a smile.

"A charming story, quite charming. A little predictable, perhaps, but I suppose that's the way of those cobwebby old tales." He smiled at the Grand Teller, who did not smile back.

"Now, to the next order of business," Lord Mortlake went on. "As a sign of our deep affection for Lady Elanor, we have prepared a special dish for her. Bring it in at once!" He clapped his hands again and his squires ran outside. They returned a few minutes later, pushing a cart. On the cart was the most enormous pie Sebastian had ever seen. His stomach rumbled loudly. Luckily, the wooden wheels of the cart made such a racket on the flagstones that nobody noticed.

Lord Mortlake drew his sword with a flourish. Everyone gasped and leaned back in alarm, but the Lord of Frostwick Castle simply used the sword to cut open the pie. Out flew a flock of white-winged doves that swooped up into the rafters. *Coo-coo*, they cried. *Coo-coo*.

One flew right over Cedric's head and, in its fright, dropped a great white splat of droppings into his hair. Cedric shrieked and began rubbing at his head with a napkin. Lady Elanor hid her smile as best she could. Mistress Mauldred hissed: "Ladies do not giggle!"

To everyone's amazement, a boy leapt out of the pie and somersaulted down to land before the high table. He then went tumbling and cartwheeling all around the room, so fast he was practically a blur. He ended with a high, double backflip, landing neatly on his feet.

"Jack Spry, at your service, Lady Elanor," he cried,

snatching off his velvet hat and bowing low. Everyone cheered and clapped.

Then the boy sang, sweet as any lark:

"Jack be nimble,

Jack be quick,

Jack jump over the candlestick.

Jack be nimble,

Jack be spry,

Jack jumps out of the apple pie!"

He was thin, about eleven years of age, with a mop of black curls and sparkling black eyes. He was dressed in a short tunic made of yellow and orange squares, with striped leggings below. On his feet were boots dyed the same vivid orange. Elanor said gravely, "Thank you, Master Spry."

The boy bowed again.

"Jack Spry is our gift to you, to be your fool and keep you entertained," Lord Mortlake said. "He can sing and dance and tell jokes and do tricks, and is a fine acrobat."

Jack Spry did another backflip, landing squarely on his feet. Everyone clapped and cheered, and he bowed to the crowd. Lord Mortlake flipped him a coin and it disappeared as if by magic.

"Let this be the beginning of a new friendship between our houses," Lord Mortlake said to Lord Wolfgang, smiling broadly.

Lord Wolfgang looked troubled. "We thank you for your kind consideration," he answered. "But—"

"So, will you give us the river rights?" Lord Mortlake interrupted.

Lord Wolfgang answered, "I am always willing to discuss terms, you know that, my lord. But this is not the time or the place. It is time for our midsummer bonfire. I hope you will join us for the dancing."

He rose and held out his arm for his daughter, who rose too. They led the way out of the great hall, the other nobles streaming behind them, laughing and chattering.

Sebastian grabbed a platter of uneaten food and rushed with it to the antechamber, where he and the other squires would quickly gobble down what they could before they had to go to the garden to serve the nobles.

From the corner of his eye, he saw a flash of yellow and orange. Curious, he looked out the door to see Jack Spry, with his boots in his hand, hurrying up the stairs to the Lord's Tower.

THE
TELL-STONES

S parks from the bonfire flew up into the starry
sky. The castle bell tolled twelve times. It was
midnight, and time for Arwen, the Grand Teller, to
read the tell-stones.

Hands shaking with excitement, Quinn walked
slowly towards the bonfire, where the Grand Teller
stood, waiting. The dancers stopped whirling and
gathered close. Lord Wolfgang and his painfully
proper daughter sat on their chairs under the oak tree.
Lady Elanor's governess stood behind her, one hand
weighing on her shoulder. She wore a huge red ring
which seemed to make her hand even heavier.

The Lord of Frostwick Castle stood some distance

away, watching with a curiosity that seemed tinged with mockery. His son stood at the banqueting table, gobbling down honey cakes.

Quinn knelt before the Grand Teller and gave her the bag of tell-stones. Arwen poured the small white pebbles out on a cloth spread under the birch tree, its branches hung with golden ribbons and yellow witcher's herb.

Arwen then drew four tell-stones at once, placing the first to the north, the second to the west, the third to the south and the final stone to the east. Quinn knew that each direction of the compass represented a different element—Earth, Water, Fire and Air—and so had a different meaning.

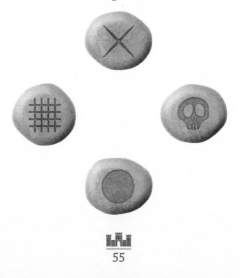

Crossroads. Gate. Dark Moon. Skull.

The Grand Teller studied the four white stones carefully. Each had a symbol painted in silver upon it. She seemed to grow pale. Quinn examined the stones too, and felt a sudden dread.

"There is danger coming," Arwen said. "Dark days lie ahead. We must all beware."

Quinn saw Tom start violently, and then flash a look at Lady Elanor. Both seemed pale and anxious, and Quinn wondered what troubled them. It was not like Tom to pay much attention to what the Grand Teller saw in her tell-stones. Though, of course, anyone would be fearful at the sign of the Skull.

"We are at a crossroads in our history. Strangers come, with dark magic and violence. There is death in the wind . . . *death* . . ." Arwen's voice rose and quickened. Her hands were clenched, her eyes wide and terrified.

"What is it?" Lord Wolfgang demanded. "What danger?"

Suddenly Arwen swayed on her feet. "Blood! I see blood! Betrayal and blood!" she cried, before collapsing in a heap. Quinn rushed to help her, Tom a few steps behind. Together they lifted the old woman to a chair, where she drooped, her head in her hand. Her face was as white as skim milk.

"Carry her to her room," Lord Wolfgang commanded, and some servants came to lift her. Once again Tom glanced meaningfully at Lady Elanor, as if wanting her to do something. Lady Elanor only looked at her father wistfully, as if wishing he would turn and look at her.

Troubled and upset, Quinn gathered up the four tell-stones and put them back in their bag.

"I am surprised you hold such old superstitions," the Lord of Frostwick said. "We got rid of our witch long ago."

"Perhaps that is why you do not prosper," the Lord of Wolfhaven replied, not tempering his words with any hint of a smile.

The Lord of Frostwick scowled. "I do not prosper because I have no river and no harbor, nor any of your fertile lands," he snapped. Then he eased his face with an effort. "I beg your pardon, I do not mean to quarrel.

We've agreed not to discuss the matter until I can find some way to raise the funds to pay all your tolls and taxes. Let us hope we all have a bountiful harvest this year."

"The only harvest will be of dragon teeth and human bones," the Grand Teller muttered, lifting her head for a moment as the servants carried her towards the old oak tree.

"What a gloomy old woman," Lord Mortlake said. "Shall we dance again? My son and I must leave at first light tomorrow, but there's no reason not to enjoy ourselves now." He clapped his hands. "Music!"

Startled, the musicians seized their pipes and drums and lyres. Music rang out, and the lords and ladies took hands to dance around the bonfire once more. As Quinn began to pack away the cloth, Tom said to her in an undertone: "Quinn, you must tell the witch that I too have had a warning. I saw the wild man of the woods . . . he told me *danger* comes . . . that the wolves smell danger in the wind!"

"Smelled something in the wind?" Quinn replied. "That was probably you."

"Quinn, stop it, please," Tom pleaded. "No one will listen to me . . . the wild man said I had to warn the lord." He made an abrupt move, as if about to charge over and accost the lord himself, and Quinn caught his arm, not wanting him to get into trouble.

"Well, the Grand Teller has told him now," she answered. "We can only hope he listened to her."

But the Lord of Wolfhaven Castle sat with his bearded chin sunk into his hands, staring at the bonfire as if recalling long ago midsummers, much brighter and merrier than this one.

MIDNIGHT ➤➤ SHIFT

"Well, I cannot see any sign of danger coming," Tom said, looking out from the castle battlements. To the west, the ocean was transformed into a golden mantle by the setting sun. To the east, twilight was sinking over the forest, and the trees were silhouetted black against the fading sky. "Unless it's that Spry kid, poking and prying into every corner of the castle. I've caught him in half a dozen places he shouldn't be."

"Jack Spry is still just finding his way around," Quinn answered. "He's had a hard life, I think. Perhaps he's had to learn to check out each new place he's in, to be sure he has an escape route."

"He asks a lot of questions too," Tom said. "He's been following me around, pestering me to know everything there is to know about the castle. Why does he do that?"

"You ask a lot of questions too," Quinn grinned. Her wild black curls blew away from her face. "Smell that wind. I wonder where it has been and what it has seen."

"The wind can't see anything."

She looked at him sideways. "How do you know?"

"It has no eyes," Tom answered impatiently.

"Do you need eyes to see, and do you need ears to hear?"

"I think being apprenticed to the witch has been very bad for you," Tom replied.

Quinn only smiled.

"I need to get back to the kitchen else Mam will be after me." Tom sighed. "Come on, Fergus." The wolfhound stood up, stretching and yawning, showing a mouth full of sharp teeth.

Quinn ruffled the wolfhound's ears. "All right, I'll stand guard now, but you need to be back before midnight."

"I'll do my best."

"No, you must come back in time. It's the night of the Dark Moon and the Grand Teller needs my help in the rituals."

"I'm sure she can manage to carry her own bag of rocks," Tom replied, and dodged Quinn's swift punch. "All right! I get the message. I'll be back by midnight."

Tom waved good-bye and ran down the steps, taking them two at a time.

"Bring me back something to eat," Quinn called after him.

When Tom came back at midnight, with some bread and cheese for Quinn, it was to find a fog creeping in from the north. It swirled down from the mountains, shrouding the roofs of the town.

"It's strange," Quinn said, rubbing her bare arms. "It's turned so cold."

Tom had brought up a blanket to sit on, and he tossed it to her. She wrapped it around herself, and stood staring to the north. Nothing could be seen of the stars now, only pale drifts of mist.

"What is the Dark One that goes over the earth,

swallows water and wood but is afraid of the wind?" she asked, so low that Tom could hardly hear her.

"What? What's the answer?" Tom demanded.

Quinn swirled one hand in the air, raising a tiny breeze which caused the mist to eddy and swirl.

"Ah," he said. "Now I get it. You mean the mist."

"He got it! Is old muttonhead growing some brains at last?" Quinn mocked.

The castle bells began to toll the midnight hour. The sound was strangely muffled. "I've got to go," said Quinn, eating the last of her bread. "Arwen will be looking for me."

"I'm not sure there's any point standing guard in the fog," Tom said. "Besides, it's been three weeks already and I'm sick of keeping watch half the night. Mam's cross with me for practically falling asleep with my head in my stew."

"The Grand Teller is unhappy with me too," Quinn answered. "She keeps asking me where I'm slipping off to all the time."

"Maybe the wild man's warning was hogwash," Tom said. After three weeks, it was hard to remember the urgency of the wild man's words and the firm grip of his fingers. Tom could only think how tired he was after days of trying to keep watch as well as do all his chores . . . while nothing unusual happened. He thought longingly of his soft, warm bed by the fire in the kitchen.

"What about the tell-stones?" urged Quinn. "And the Grand Teller's vision?"

"Maybe they're warnings of things in coming *years*," Tom said. "It could be a long way off, and we're wearing ourselves out in the meantime. Perhaps we're better off getting some sleep so that we're alert and ready for anything that comes."

If it ever does . . . he thought to himself.

Quinn stared into the darkness. "I don't know," she answered slowly. "I don't like this fog. It . . . it feels wrong. It smells wrong."

Then Fergus growled deep in his throat. "What is it, boy?" Tom asked. The wolfhound's growl deepened into a snarl. He put both paws up onto the battlement, sniffing the wind. Then he barked a warning.

Tom looked all around, but it was pitch-black and impossible to see a thing.

A distant rattle and creak made him spin and look down into the inner ward. A gust of wind carried a strange smell, like marsh gas, and swirled the mist away.

He saw a dark, hooded figure dragging open the war gate. It was so heavy that the figure had to heave and drag it with all of their strength. An immense black key jutted from the keyhole.

As soon as the gate was open, strange, dark, bony things crept through. Tom leaned forward, watching in horror. Quinn gasped and gripped the battlement beside him. The figures scuttled across the courtyard, slithered through doorways and leapt up steps. They were thin and bent, like long-legged insects, with empty eye sockets. Each carried a spear in one hand, and was preceded by a swirl of dank-smelling mist. The only sound was the soft slap of their bare feet on the stone.

Quickly, cries of alarm and shouts of terror broke out. Castle guards ran to grapple with the invaders, who fought silently, stabbing with their spears. Still more of them came through the mist, rank after rank after rank of them, eyeless and flesh-less and noiseless. It was eerie and frightening. Then, knights on great horses rode in through the open gateway, helmets pulled down over their faces. Even the horses' faces and bodies were covered with armor, while their hooves were ghostly quiet. The helmet of the leader had two up-curving boar tusks.

"Who are they?" Quinn cried. "Look, there are hundreds of them!"

"Come on!" Tom cried. "We have to sound the alarm!"

Tom ran along the battlements, shouting out at the top of his voice. "Beware, beware! Wake up! Invaders in the castle! Wake up!" Fergus loped beside him, barking. Quinn ran the other way, shouting too. But their voices were lost in the mist.

Tom raced for the bell tower. He reached through an archway, and seized hold of the bell ropes, yanking on them with all his strength. The bells rang out. Tom kept pulling at the ropes until his arms ached so fiercely he could not pull any more. Then Quinn was beside him again, taking over. The cacophony of the bells filled Tom's head, making his senses swim. His palms stung fiercely. At last, panting, Quinn had to stop too.

"The Grand Teller, I have to warn the Grand Teller!" she cried.

"Mam!"

Both ran as fast as they could along the battlements, the wolfhound swift at their heels. They reached the Lady's Tower and half fell down the steps into the keep. As they ran along the corridor, they saw a swirl of dank mist, and smelled again that strange marshy scent. Then they heard a girl's scream.

"Lady Elanor!" Tom cried.

Tom and Quinn ran to her room. Elanor was backed up against the paneling, wildly swinging a poker. She was dressed only in a chemise, her golden-brown hair tied in a long braid, her feet bare. Facing her was a crowd of the terrifying silent creatures. They seemed to be made of ancient leather wrapped tightly over bone. They looked at Tom with their empty eye sockets, nostrils flaring. They caught his scent and leapt towards him, raking the air with their nails.

Fergus leapt past Tom with a snarl. He knocked down one of the leathery creatures, which then sought to stab him with its spear. Fergus seized it in his jaws and pulled. The two had a tug-of-war, until suddenly the leather man let go, falling backward.

Meanwhile, Tom managed to grab a jug of flowers from the table and hurl it at another. It hit the target in the face then crashed to the floor, giving Tom and Quinn time to rush across to where Elanor stood, waving the poker around.

"Quick, through the secret door," Tom gasped. "Where is the key?"

Elanor darted across to where her clothes were folded over a chair, her golden slippers laid out neatly below. She grabbed them and pulled the key out of the pocket of her dress, tossing it to Tom. Fergus was rolling on the floor with another of the leathery creatures, snarling and biting and clawing. Quinn was holding off the rest with the poker, using it a lot more forcefully than Elanor had. Tom unlocked the secret door and Elanor scrambled through, her dress and shoes in her arms. Tom and Quinn were quick to follow, then Tom whistled for the wolfhound. Fergus leapt through the tiny door and Tom slammed it shut and locked it seconds before the leather men reached it. They heard the nerve-shredding scrape of nails against the wood, and turned and ran. Down the narrow spiral steps they hurtled, crashing into the walls in the darkness.

Somewhere above them, Tom heard the crack and splinter of breaking wood, and then the swift *slap, slap, slap* of leathery feet.

"Run!" he cried.

8

← « THE
TUSKED KNIGHT »→

Tom led the way down the stairs at breakneck speed and raced into the kitchen, Fergus and the two girls at his heels.

Mistress Pippin was fighting off leather men with a frying pan. "Take that, you monster, take that!" she cried. "And that!"

As one leather man crumpled to the floor, another two advanced. Slowly the cook was being forced back towards the fireplace. Fury swelled through Tom. He leapt forward, wrenched a copper pan from a hook, and began wielding it fiercely. *Thwack, crack!* Another leather man toppled to the floor, and then another. Fergus leapt on the back of one, forcing it to the ground, while Quinn took up a basket of apples and began pelting them. *Thud, thump, splat!* Then one apple, thrown rather wildly, fell into the ashes of the fire and sent up a great burst of sparks. The leather men reeled back. Tom was able to knock out one, then another, with his pan. Quinn felled one with her basket, while Mistress Pippin took care of the rest with her frying pan.

They lay twisted on the ground, all bones and leather and hair, looking like something a giant owl spat up. Tom and Quinn gingerly seized the leather men's stiff, contorted arms and dragged them out the door, locking and bolting it behind them.

"Tom," his mother cried, dropping the frying pan and holding her arms wide.

"Mam!"

They hugged each other close. Wiping away tears, Mistress Pippin pulled herself away. "I'm so glad you're safe! Quinn, dear girl, you too." She then saw Elanor, white-faced and frightened, and bobbed a surprised curtsey. "My lady, are you hurt? What on earth are you doing down here in the kitchen?"

"They . . . I . . ." Elanor stammered.

"Those leather men were trying to take her," Tom said. "Mam, what are we to do? They're everywhere!"

"You need to get away from here as fast as you can," his mother answered. She plucked a knapsack from a hook by the door and began hurling things into it—a frying pan, a pot, a wooden spoon, a round cheese in red wax, apples, a bag of dried peas, a hank of air-dried bacon and a tinderbox. Quinn hurried to help her, while Elanor quickly pulled on her green gown and golden slippers. Tom filled a waterskin from the water barrel, and grabbed some small pork pies from a plate on the table and threw them in the knapsack.

"Quick, Tom, look in the larder, behind the barrel of brine." As Mistress Pippin spoke, she took her own brown woolly shawl and wrapped it around Elanor's shoulders. Elanor huddled into it gratefully.

Tom did as he was told and found a longbow and a quiver of gray-fletched arrows, with a tightly rolled gray cloak tied to it.

"The bow belonged to your father when he was a boy. I've been saving it for you. You must go to him, he will help us," Mistress Pippin said, hurriedly shoving a small pouch of coins into the knapsack.

"My father?" Tom was flabbergasted. "But where?"

"Look for him in the forest where the wolves howl." Mistress Pippin took her wedding ring off and thrust it in Tom's hand. He knew it well. Made of fine gold, it was in the shape of two hands holding a heart. "Wear it, keep it safe. He'll know it when he sees it."

"But Mam . . . my father . . . I don't even know his name," said Tom, sliding the ring on his middle finger.

"He's called Hunter. That's what he was, you know. He was the Lord's Wolf Catcher once . . . a long time ago. But . . . you must get away." As she spoke, Mistress Pippin was hurriedly filling another knapsack for Quinn to carry.

"But Mam, what does he look like? Where will I find him?"

"In the forest, I told you. And what does he look

like?" Her face softened and she patted Tom's cheek. "You have his eyes, Tomkin."

Just then, someone began trying to kick down the kitchen door. Everyone jumped. Elanor screamed.

"Shhh, shh, sweetling, we need to hide you. Into the larder, quick." Mistress Pippin raised her frying pan.

"Into the larder?" Quinn cried.

"Yes, yes. There's a secret way out through there. Climb over those barrels, press the stone at the back, the one with a little hollow . . . that's the one."

Over the sound of the banging at the door, Tom heard a click as a stone in the wall of the larder swung aside. Quinn went through eagerly, and Elanor and Tom followed close behind. Tom whistled softly to Fergus to follow.

"Mam, hurry," Tom said, as the banging at the door grew louder. His mother was just about to follow him when suddenly the kitchen door broke down, and a tall figure in black armor strode through, a sword in his hand. His helmet had boar tusks on it.

Fergus growled, but Tom grabbed his collar and held him back, putting his hand over the dog's muzzle to keep him quiet. From the shadows of the larder, he could just see more men in armor crowding into the kitchen. At once, Mistress Pippin stood in front of the larder door, her frying pan held high.

"How dare you burst into my kitchen like that!" she cried. "Have you no manners, you knave?"

"Where is the little lady?" the knight growled menacingly.

"I have no idea what you're talking about," Mistress Pippin answered. Behind her back, she gestured urgently for Tom to go, but he couldn't bear to leave her.

The knight strode forward, putting the point of his sword to Mistress Pippin's throat. "Lady Elanor. Where is she?"

Tom jerked forward, but Quinn held him desperately, one small hand covering his mouth. "Shhh," she whispered in his ear.

"Tucked up, sound asleep in her bed, no doubt, which is where I'd like to be," Mistress Pippin answered. "Now get that nasty sharp thing out of my face!"

The knight threw back his head and laughed. It

sounded weird and horrible booming through the metal of his tusked helmet. Tom saw that his sword had a handle of bone, all carved with strange symbols. The man put the point of his sword to the floor and leaned on it, slowly pulling off one gauntlet. He wore a huge red ring on one finger.

"I don't *want* to hurt you. My bog-men have traced her scent here. Tell me where she has gone and we will send you to the dungeons with the others. Refuse to tell me and . . ." The knight slapped his gauntlet into his bare hand.

"*Bog-men?*" Tom murmured. To his horror, a swarm of them crept forward, sniffing the flagstones.

His mother flapped her hand urgently behind her back. "No need to get nasty," she said. "I don't know why you're looking for her here. Ladies don't come down to the kitchen."

Once more she gestured emphatically behind her back. With a choke in his throat, Tom let Quinn pull him into the passageway. As Quinn dragged the secret door closed, Mistress Pippin whacked the knight hard over the head with her frying pan.

9

BATTLE WITH THE BOG-MEN

Elanor could hardly see a thing. She stumbled forward, almost tripping on her skirts and falling.

Quinn whispered to Tom. "Are you all right?"

"I'm fine," he answered, dashing his arm across his eyes. "I just . . . I just hope they don't hurt Mam."

"She's so brave," Quinn whispered back.

"She may be small, but she's fierce." Tom's voice cracked.

They hurried down a dark passage, lit only by the occasional slash of light through a crack in the stone. Fergus was running ahead, his nose to the ground. When he turned, looking for Tom, his eyes glowed green. Through the wall came the muffled sounds of battle—clangs, screams and cries—then, horribly close, through a crack in the stone, a sniffling, snuffling sound.

They all ran as quietly as they could in the dimness. The passageway turned sharply, then went up spiral stairs as steep as a ladder. Elanor scrambled up, gasping for breath. She had never run so far or fast in her life.

"Where does this lead us?" Quinn whispered, as the steps wound higher and higher into darkness.

"I have no idea," Tom whispered back. "But we can't go back, we must keep going forward."

They passed a small alcove and Tom suddenly stopped. "There's a door here. Shall we see where it leads?" Without waiting for an answer, he turned the handle and swung the door open. It creaked. Tom stopped, then, very slowly, eased it open wider. It creaked more loudly. He stepped through, Fergus pushing past him. "All's clear," he whispered.

Quinn crept through, and Elanor followed. She found herself in a part of the castle she did not recognize. It was a round room, with a huge fireplace at one end, and narrow window slits breaking up the stone walls. Once the secret door swung shut, it was impossible to see where it was. Elanor wondered how many other secret doors there were in the castle.

Rushes covered the floor, and the walls were hung with all sorts of weapons. "The guard room," Tom whispered in surprise. "Quick, let's arm ourselves while we can." He took down a dagger in a scabbard and tossed it to Quinn, who swiftly belted it to her waist, on the opposite side to her black witch's knife. Tom found another dagger for Elanor.

"Oh, no, I couldn't," she protested, pushing the dagger away with both hands.

"You must," Quinn replied fiercely, taking the dagger from Tom and thrusting it into Elanor's hands. "You may have to fight, my lady, else we'll all be taken captive."

Ladies don't fight, her governess said in her mind. But Elanor was doing many things of which her governess would not approve. She took the dagger and strapped it to her golden belt with shaking hands.

Tom took a dagger for himself, and grabbed a coil of rope. Then, with an effort that made him grunt and grow red in the face, he bent and strung the longbow, and put an arrow to it.

"Can you shoot?" Quinn asked him.

"Not very well," he answered. "Though every time I go to the forest I practice best I can, with an old bow and arrows I made myself." He raised the bow and arrow, and squinted along the arrow. "This is much better."

"Anything else we should take?" Quinn asked. "We might have to fight our way out."

A shudder ran over Elanor.

"You should have shoes, Quinn," Tom said, looking at the witch girl's bare feet. "The forest is filled with thorns, thistles and sharp stones."

Quinn raised her chin. "A witch draws power from the earth. I can never cut myself off from that."

"Fine. Can you do anything useful with that power? Summon a fireball or two, or make us invisible?"

"Magic doesn't work that way."

"Of course it doesn't. Well, then, what *can* you do?"

"Lots of stuff," Quinn snapped. "Stuff a thickhead

like you could never understand."

"Well, mutter a spell or two and get us out of here!" Tom snapped back.

Quinn's face was white. "I wish I could. If only I was ready to find my witch's staff . . . but until I do, I can do nothing. Oh, Tom, we need to go and see the Grand Teller. Arwen will know what to do."

"We can't," he said shortly. "We need to get out of here as fast as we can."

Quinn and Tom stared at each other angrily, then she tossed back her thick mane of curly hair and began to run out of the room. "Coming?" she mocked over her shoulder. Tom raced after her, and overtook her on the steps, Fergus bounding along beside him. Elanor followed timidly.

As they hurried down the steps towards the inner ward, Quinn turned to Elanor, her narrow face full of sympathy. "I know you're afraid," she whispered. "But fear is the worst of your enemies. Try and be brave."

Elanor swallowed hard, and nodded.

As they descended the staircase, the sound of fighting grew louder. They came to the doorway and peeked out into the courtyard. Armored knights battled against castle guards. The bog-men scuttled around, spears thrusting mercilessly. Mist roiled everywhere, turning orange here and there where flaming torches had been stuck in brackets on the walls.

"We have to sneak past," Tom whispered. "Let's head for the garden gate. I know where the spare key is kept."

They crept out the door and along the wall, keeping close together. Tom kept his hand on Fergus's collar. They had almost reached the archway that led to the garden when Elanor saw a mass of Wolfhaven folk being herded through the inner keep towards the dungeons, guarded by unknown knights. They were bound together by chains, manacles gripping their wrists and ankles. Sir Kevyn was fighting every step of the way, four knights struggling to hold him back. The chamberlain was crawling along on his knees, imploring the bog-men to keep away. Mistress Pippin's face was grim and bruised. She struggled to free herself of the two men who held her. Then, with horror, Elanor saw her own father, Lord Wolfgang, chained and manacled like the rest. "Father," she whimpered.

At once, one of the bog-men raised his head and sniffed. His eyeless head swiveled towards her, then he began to run. *Slap, slap, slap*, went his feet on the stone. *Sniff, sniff, sniff*, went his flaring nostrils.

"Tom," Elanor cried. "Help!"

Tom bent his bow and sent an arrow whizzing into the bog-man's shoulder. The creature simply pulled it out and kept running towards them. Quinn jumped in front of Elanor, pulling free her dagger and her black witch's knife. Tom fitted another arrow to his bow.

Then another boy leapt in front of the bog-man, and his sword flashed down. A withered arm spun away into the darkness. The bog-man lurched on, now armless. The boy made another desperate swipe. He sliced off one of the bog-man's legs. The creature fell and could not rise, but wriggled forward, reaching for Elanor's ankle. She screamed and scrambled away.

On hearing her scream, all the bog-men's heads whipped around. They began to lope towards her. The boy jumped in front of her, using his sword to chop off the crawling bog-man's head. At last, the creature went still.

Tom raised his bow, firing arrow after arrow into the bog-men. They simply pulled the arrows out and kept running. Quinn bent and picked up the spear the dead creature had dropped, and flung it as hard as she could. It went straight through the empty eye socket of one of the attackers, and he fell silently. Fergus snarled and leapt, taking down another. The unknown boy's sword flashed as he swiped it sideways. It got snagged in the neck of one of the bog-men. The boy grunted and tried to pull his sword free, but then more of the beasts were upon him, spears raised high. He lifted his shield, protecting his neck and shoulders. It was emblazoned with the writhing shape of a red dragon.

Tom jumped up and pulled one of the flaming torches from the wall. He swiped it from side to side. The bog-men leapt back. Tom pursued them with the torch, and they retreated, giving Quinn time to help drag back the boy who had helped them fight. His hair gleamed red under the flare of the torches, and Elanor recognized him at once. He was Lord Sebastian Byrne, the squire who had tumbled into her bedchamber on the night she had met Tom.

"Oh, it's you," Tom said, unenthusiastically.

"You!" Sebastian cried. "If I had known it was you, pot boy, I wouldn't have—"

Just then, the torch in Tom's hand began to splutter and smoke. The bog-men surged forward.

Tom threw the dying torch in their faces. "Run!"

Through the archway they raced, and along the narrow passageway into the inner ward. Bog-men loped after them, spears held high. The four children swerved, spun, ran and sidestepped, bog-men hot on their heels. It was like a mad game of mob-ball. Whenever they passed a torch, one or other of the children would grab it and fling it back at their relentless pursuers. Each time, the creatures flinched and retreated, but it only gained them a few seconds.

As Elanor and Tom ran towards the shelter of the

garden, they collided with someone in the darkness. He went down with a great clang, and dropped the sack he was carrying. Quinn ran up, a flaming torch in her hand. The light fell upon the pale face of Jack Spry, and glittered upon the silver plates and candlesticks that had rolled out of his sack. The boy scooped them back up and thrust them into his sack. "Watch where you're going," he growled at Tom, before running off towards the garden gate.

"Wait! They're my father's candlesticks!" Elanor cried. But Jack Spry had disappeared into the darkness.

A spear whizzed past Tom's head. Quinn waved the flaming torch at the bog-men, keeping them back, as Sebastian swung his sword wildly. Fergus snarled and lunged. The smell of the marshes was strong. The bog-men closed in on them once more, waiting for the torch to sizzle and go out.

"What do we do?" Elanor asked, the dagger shaking in her hands.

"We'll never make it to the gate," Tom panted.

"The Grand Teller's house," Quinn gasped. "This way!"

They flung the torch into the bog-men's faces then turned and ran towards the immense oak tree that grew like a gnarled giant in the center of the garden. The tree's branches were hung with tiny, paper lanterns, like fireflies.

Suddenly a tiny door in the trunk of the tree swung open, casting out a fan of radiance. The Grand Teller stood there, beckoning them inside, her silver hair hanging loose down her back. Four children and one big dog raced past her. The Grand Teller then banged on the ground with her tall staff, and suddenly every paper lantern on the tree burst into flame. The bog-men fell back. The door slammed shut.

Thud, thud, thud. Spears hammered the door. Elanor, looking around the small room inside the tree's trunk, realized with horror that they were trapped.

THE GRAND TELLER'S TREE

"Our only hope is to wake the sleeping heroes," the Grand Teller said, rummaging around on a high shelf.

"What?" Sebastian cried. "You can't be serious. That's just an old wives' tale."

Arwen looked at him quizzically. "There's much truth in old tales." She found a carved chest and began to lift it down. Sebastian went to help her, for he was taller than she was, even though he was only thirteen. "Thank you, Lord Sebastian," she said. "You may put the chest on the table."

Arwen looked at the group of children, crowded together in the tiny room. Tom was passing around the waterskin.

"I meant what I said," Arwen urged. "Our only hope is to wake the sleeping heroes. There's an old spell I've kept close for many years, in fear of just this day."

"What day?" Tom demanded. "What's happening? Who are those leathery creatures? And who is the tusked knight? Why are they attacking us?"

"I do not know," the Grand Teller answered. "Enemies, that is for sure. I have had troubling omens this last moon, but nothing clear. I warned Lord Wolfgang, but he would not listen."

"How did they get in?" Sebastian asked. "I thought the castle was impenetrable."

Arwen looked shrunken and old. "I fear treachery . . ." she whispered under her breath.

Another round of blows on the door echoed through the room. Sebastian's spine stiffened. Those deadly creatures made him feel sick. They didn't seem to care about having their arms and legs chopped off. And the way they sniffed the air! If he had not been a knight-in-training, Sebastian would have shuddered at the thought.

The wolfhound ran to the door, growling. Then he barked loudly as another blow hit the wood. "Shhh, Fergus," Tom said, clicking his fingers. The wolfhound went to his side, growling low. Sebastian imagined the bog-men out there, with only a wooden door between their sharp spears and him. He was the only one who really knew how to fight. It would be up to him to hold them off, if they were to break in.

He looked around, wondering if there was any way to escape. The room was roundish in shape, with gnarled and knobbly walls of living wood. Natural cavities and shelves were filled with books, boxes, and jars of seeds, feathers and shells. On the floor was a round handwoven rug in reds and browns. A small stove was set against one curved wall, with a metal chimney rising up through the ceiling.

Beside a rocking chair was an odd round basket made of willow twigs. A tabby cat stood on a cushion inside the basket, back arched, spitting in warning. Quinn picked it up, soothing its fur with one hand. She rocked the basket with one bare foot, saying to Tom, "This is mine, you know. It's the basket I was found in."

"You must've been tiny," Tom said.

She nodded, looking sad.

An owl was perched on the chair's back, its ear tufts erect, its feathers ruffled. It stared at Sebastian with round, golden eyes and he stared back. He had never seen an owl so close.

The only clear way out of the room was a ladder that led to a floor above. Sebastian wondered if there was any way out from there.

The banging on the door intensified. Suddenly the wood cracked. The children all jumped.

"Do not fear," the witch said, opening the chest. "The door will hold another minute or two. Now listen to me carefully. You must remember what the spell says." She unrolled an ancient-looking parchment and read it, in a voice that quavered.

WHEN THE WOLF LIES DOWN WITH THE WOLFHOUND
AND THE STONES OF THE CASTLE SING,
THE SLEEPING HEROES SHALL WAKE FOR THE CROWN
AND THE BELLS OF VICTORY RING.

Elanor stared at the parchment. "But what does it mean? Wolves don't lie down with wolfhounds." Fergus gave a small growl as if to say they certainly did not.

"And stones don't sing," Tom said. "Surely it's just a nonsense rhyme, like the ones they sing to babies."

"There's a lot of sense in nonsense rhymes," the Grand Teller said.

"But how are we to make it happen, Arwen?" Quinn asked. "We have a wolfhound." She patted Fergus on the head. "Do we just need to find a wolf? That shouldn't be too hard."

"Making Fergus lie down next to a wolf will be," Tom said.

"And how are we meant to make the stones sing?" Sebastian demanded. "It's a bag of moonshine!"

Arwen continued reading, slowly.

GRIFFIN FEATHER AND UNICORN'S HORN,
SEA SERPENT SCALE AND DRAGON'S TOOTH,
BRING THEM TOGETHER AT FIRST LIGHT OF DAWN,
AND YOU SHALL SEE THIS SPELL'S TRUTH.

The children stared at her blankly.

"But that's impossible," Sebastian burst out. "There are no such things as dragons and griffins and unicorns and sea serpents. They only exist in stories!"

"Haven't I told you already that there's a lot of truth in old tales?" asked Arwen. "Have you not been listening? You need to listen if you are to learn, Lord Sebastian."

He went red and crossed his arms. "It's a wild goose chase you're sending us on. An impossible quest!"

"The world is full of magical things, waiting for us to greet them," the Grand Teller replied. "You shall not see them with a closed heart."

In the silence that followed, the banging on the door intensified. Someone out there had found an ax, and was chopping at a crack in the door. Fergus whimpered, his tail tucked between his legs.

"Even if such beasts were real, how are we meant to catch them?" Elanor said in a frightened voice.

"If you are brave of heart, sharp of wit, strong of spirit and steadfast of purpose, there is nothing you cannot achieve," the Grand Teller answered. "But come. I cannot keep them out much longer. It is the darkest hour of the night and my strength is ebbing. I have some gifts for you."

Arwen quickly unknotted the oaken medallion she wore around her neck, carved with the face of an old man surrounded by leaves. She passed it to Quinn. "He is carved from bog oak and is many thousands of years old. He will help you to be wise."

Quinn hung the medallion around her neck, as Arwen passed her the small bag of tell-stones. "Take care of them and bring them back to me," she said. Quinn nodded, her turquoise green eyes bright with tears. Arwen then opened a chest and drew out a soft white shawl, as lacy as a cobweb. "This is yours," she said. "You were found wrapped in it. It's light, but it will keep you warm."

As Quinn gratefully accepted the shawl, the Grand Teller gave a ring to Elanor. "It's a moonstone. It's called the Traveler's Stone for it protects those that travel, whether by night or day, by land or sea, or in their dreams. It will help keep you safe."

"Thank you." Elanor slipped the ring on, and the stone glowed, round as the eye of a daisy, and set in small silver petals.

The Grand Teller then handed Sebastian a cloak pin carved from golden-hued wood, in the shape of a dragon curled around a lump of amber. "This is carved from wood from the rowan tree," Arwen said. "Rowan wood is a powerful protection from evil."

Sebastian nodded and pinned the wooden dragon to his jacket.

Finally, Arwen tossed Tom a small wooden flute. "It's made from the wood of the elder tree," she began, but just then an ax chopped a great hole through the door.

"Tom," she cried urgently, while rolling back her rug, "elder wood is very magical indeed. Use it wisely." Beneath the rug was a trapdoor. The old woman swung it open, revealing a set of steep steps leading down into darkness. She grabbed a lantern from the table and passed it to Tom, who thrust the flute into his pocket and snatched up his knapsack and bow and arrows. "The steps lead down to the harbor. Hurry! You must turn left, left, right, left, left, right, till you reach the Great Cave. Then just follow the water. Be careful. This mountain is riddled with dangerous caves and passageways. You do not want to get lost!"

Tom climbed down the steps, whistling for Fergus, who bounded past him, almost knocking him over. Elanor followed, looking white and frightened. Sebastian turned to beckon Quinn to hurry. She was hesitating, looking back at the old witch, her knapsack slung over one shoulder. The door was breaking apart under the onslaught of axes.

"Aren't you coming with us?"

"I'm too old for such adventures," Arwen said. "Besides, I must stay and see what I can do to help here. There'll be people wounded, frightened—"

"But the bog-men," Quinn pleaded, "they'll hurt you."

"Not I," Arwen replied. "Go, my sweet girl. Remember what I have taught you. Remember the spell. Don't fail me."

Quinn rubbed away her tears and climbed down the steps. Sebastian grasped his sword tightly, his shield hooked over one arm, and followed close behind her. The trapdoor thumped down above his head, and he was left groping his way down in darkness. Far below his feet, he could see the feeble glow of Tom's lantern, shining through coiling snake-like roots.

Sebastian gulped. He did not like small dark spaces. But there had to be a way out, he told himself. He squared his shoulders and kept climbing down.

But the steps kept winding down, down, down, and soon Sebastian's legs were aching. He heard Elanor's breath coming in little gasps and wondered if she was crying.

A long time later, Tom's voice came wavering

through the gloom. "We've reached a passageway. At last. Did she say to turn left or right? I can't remember."

"I don't remember either," Elanor quavered.

"Left," Quinn said.

"Right," Sebastian said.

"It was left," Quinn insisted, impatiently.

"Right," Tom replied. "Sorry, I mean, yes, fine, *left* it is."

The light veered to the left.

"Who put *you* in charge?" said Sebastian furiously, at last reaching the bottom of the steps.

"I'm the one with the light," came the distant answer. "Feel free to turn right if you want!"

The light went on down the left-hand passageway, growing dimmer till it disappeared.

Sebastian stumped after it, promising himself he would pummel that pot boy to pieces the very first chance he got.

THE CAVE OF »———→
←———« ICICLES

S tumbling with weariness, Quinn followed the small bobbing light. The passageway branched again and again, sometimes winding through rock, sometimes leading down steep, crude steps, sometimes opening up into caverns where old chests were piled in heaps against the walls.

Left, left, right, she repeated endlessly in her mind. *Left, left, right.* But other words broke her concentration. *Griffin . . . unicorn . . . dragon . . . sea serpent . . . sleeping heroes . . . an impossible quest . . .* She wondered if they would pass through the cavern where the sleeping heroes were lying. How long had they been there, asleep? Would their hair and beards have grown tremendously long? Would they be spun with cobwebs, or shrouded with dust? Perhaps their clothes would be moth-eaten, or nibbled to pieces by mice. In her imagination, Quinn saw them, gray and stern and forbidding. She imagined trying to wake them, imagined their anger. Then she stumbled and almost fell.

Take care, little maid. The dark is deep and the way is long, and once thou art lost, the way will be gone.

The voice that spoke to her was low and weary, the voice of an old, old man. Quinn started with surprise, and looked around her.

There was no old man to be seen.

Quinn realized with a sudden chill that she had been walking in a daze, hardly aware of her surroundings.

The bobbing light had paused at a junction. "Which way?" Tom asked. His eyes were very blue in his dirty face.

Had they gone left last time, or right? Quinn couldn't remember. She thought of all the times her mind had wandered in her weariness. Had she missed a turnoff? Had they gone the wrong way?

"It's left this time," Sebastian said.

"I think it's left too," Elanor said. "I am sure we only turned left once since we last turned right."

"No, it's *right*," Tom said. "I've been keeping track."

"Then why did you ask Quinn?" Sebastian demanded.

"I just wanted to be sure," Tom answered.

Elanor looked from one to another. Her forehead was drawn down into an anxious knot.

Once thou art lost, the way will be gone, the old, tired voice said again.

"I don't know the way," Quinn said, hearing the panic in her own voice. "I'm sorry."

Tom drew his dagger, and used it to scrape four narrow marks on the wall.

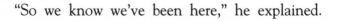

"So we know we've been here," he explained.

"We'll explore one way and then the other, till we find a sign we've gone astray."

Then, after a lot more argument, they turned left. The passageway wound on a long way, but then led into a small cave with a stone shelf where an ancient blanket lay rotting. Chained to the walls were some manacles.

"No bones," Tom said, poking the old blanket with his dagger. "That's good."

Quinn couldn't bear the thought of some prisoner being left down here in the darkness. She backed away from the room. "Come on, we have to find the right way again."

"Are we lost?" Elanor asked.

"Just a little detour," Sebastian reassured her.

"I told you we should have turned right," Tom said.

They all walked on in silence.

"I'm thirsty," Elanor said.

Tom passed her the waterskin. One gulp and it was all gone. Quinn was thirsty too. She hoped they would find more water soon.

"I'm so tired," Elanor said after a while. "Can

we stop a while?"

"The lantern's guttering," Tom answered. "It'll soon go out."

Everyone's steps quickened.

At last the passageway opened out into a vast cavern, hung with what looked like thousands of icicles. When Quinn touched one, she realized it was not made of ice, but rather some kind of damp, pale stone. Below, more stone icicles grew up out of the slippery stone floor. In some places the two met, forming weirdly shaped columns and arches, colored in all shades of white, cream, yellow and blue. Fergus whined, his tail tucked out of sight. Tom lifted his lantern high, but there was only yawning darkness above them. Water tinkled somewhere.

"This must be the Great Cave," Quinn cried. Her voice echoed strangely. "Now all we need to do is follow the water." Fergus leapt forward, and led them to a narrow stream. He bent his shaggy head and lapped thirstily. All four children bent and scooped up water in their hands. They were too thirsty to worry about how clean the water was. It was icy and tasted a little metallic, but they gulped it down eagerly, and Tom refilled the waterskin.

Then they hurried on, keeping close together in the bitterly cold darkness, following the stream. Quinn's bare feet felt frozen, and she was grateful for the warmth of the white shawl around her shoulders.

The stream wound along the floor of the cavern, carving its way through the soft, slippery stone. Elanor shrieked as she slipped sideways and splashed into the stream. Sebastian tried to yank her out and fell hard on his backside. Quinn only saved herself by grabbing at one of the stone icicles. When Tom tried to pull Sebastian up, his feet slipped out from under him and down he went again. Sebastian got up, rubbing himself and looking furious.

"You did that on purpose," he said to Tom.

"I didn't, I promise," Tom replied, trying not to laugh.

Sebastian pushed him and Tom stumbled back into the stream.

"Now my boots are wet! Thanks a lot." He squelched out of the stream and would have shoved Sebastian back if Quinn had not said, "Stop it, you two. If you break a leg you'll be stuck down here."

The thought of being trapped in the cold and dark sobered them all, and they hurried as fast as they could along the stream, as the light in the lantern sank lower and lower.

The stream slowly grew deeper and wider, running swiftly over the rocks in small cascades. They followed it, scrambling and slipping, until it widened out into a blue-green lake that filled the far end of the cavern. The stone icicles framed it like delicate lace.

Bobbing up and down in the water was a small brown boat, tied to a stone column. Round golden eyes had been painted on either side of the prow, which was carved to look like an owl's beak.

"What on earth is a boat doing here, on a lake so deep underground?" Tom cried.

"It's odd," Elanor said. "I don't like it."

"Perhaps the boat is for us, to help us escape," Quinn said. She lifted up her white skirts and stepped into the water. "Ow! This water's freezing." She waded towards the boat and grasped the rope, pulling the vessel towards her.

"I don't think you should do that," Sebastian said.

Quinn leaned over and pulled out a thick brown blanket. "There are cushions and blankets inside," she said, sniffing the blanket. "It doesn't smell damp at all."

"We could rest in there for a while," Tom said. "Much better than sitting on the damp, cold rocks." He sat on a rock and took off his wet boots.

"I don't know," Sebastian said. "Maybe it's a trap."

"A trap set by who?" Tom jeered, as he splashed towards the boat, holding the dying lantern high, his boots in his other hand. He put one hand on the side, holding it steady, then leapt in. "Mmmm, warm. Come on, Lady Elanor. Aren't you cold and tired?"

"Indeed, I am," she agreed, still hesitating.

Quinn had already clambered aboard, and was sighing in relief as she sank down on one of the cushioned seats. "Come on," she said. "There's no need to fear. Can't you see this boat must belong to Arwen?"

Elanor and Sebastian hesitated.

"Besides," Quinn said, holding high the knapsack, "*we* have all the food."

12

THE BOAT WITH OWL EYES

Quinn laughed as Sebastian instantly sat down to take off his long boots and stockings, rolling his leather leggings to above the knee. Elanor took off her slippers and kilted up her silken skirt, and Sebastian helped her through the icy water to the boat.

"I thought the food would persuade you," Quinn said. She saw a small locker to one side and opened it. "Look, here's another lantern," Quinn said. "We won't be in the dark after all."

She took Tom's lantern, which had almost spluttered out, and managed to light the fresh lantern with a long taper she found in the cupboard. Light flared up, showing for an instant just how immense the cavern was. Then it settled down, filling the boat with a warm glow. Tom refilled his lantern and hung it at the back of the boat, as the other two clambered in and made themselves comfortable.

Then Tom whistled for Fergus.

The wolfhound ran back and forth on the shore, whining, then evidently decided he must risk the lake. He galloped towards the boat, sending up great sprays of water, then leapt in. The boat rocked wildly as he landed.

"Fergus!" Quinn moaned. "Must you?"

The dog grinned happily, then shook himself violently. Water flicked all over the four children. They all groaned and hid their faces, till Fergus at last settled down at their feet.

"Is there any smell worse than wet dog?" Sebastian said, leaning as far away from Fergus as he could get.

"Yes. Wet boy," Quinn replied at once, holding her nose and leaning away from Sebastian. He grimaced at her and she laughed.

"How about some food?" Tom said. "I don't know about you, but I'm starving."

They investigated the knapsacks, and found bread, cold sausages, pork pies, apples and currant buns. All four fell upon the food with gusto. It had been a long and exhausting night. Fergus ate a whole pie and five sausages by himself, then begged tidbits from each in turn.

Once they had eaten their fill, they put the remains of the feast back in the knapsacks.

"We'd better get moving," Quinn said, forcing herself to get up from her warm and comfortable position. She undid the rope, and used an oar to push the boat away from the shore.

Sebastian sat up. "What are you doing?"

"Seeing where the boat takes us, of course."

The boat spun out, and was quickly caught by a current.

Sebastian gripped the sides of the boat as it gathered speed. "I'm not sure that was a good idea," he said. "We don't know what lies ahead!"

Quinn smiled. "Isn't that half the fun of it? Anyway, Arwen must use this boat herself, so we know it can't go anywhere too dangerous."

"But she probably uses magic to keep it under control," Sebastian retorted.

The boat was now racing down a narrow river. The walls of the cavern loomed close on either side, the sharp stone icicles hanging right above the children's heads.

"Look out!" Quinn yelled. "Duck!"

Tom ducked, just avoiding smashing his head on a rock.

"We're going too fast," Elanor cried. "Can't we slow down?"

A great pillar of rock was right in their way.

"Lie low!" Sebastian ordered. He seized an oar, and pushed the boat away from the pillar. The boat swerved and spun, and banged against the far wall. Fergus whimpered, pressing against Tom's leg. Tom pushed him away. He had seized the other oar and, pushing with all his strength, managed to shove the boat away from the wall. It steadied, speeding along once more.

"There's a curve ahead," Quinn said.

Together the two boys worked their oars. They

surged around the corner, and saw before them a heavy iron grate, with water gleaming faintly beyond.

"We're going to crash!" Elanor shouted, crouching down in the bottom of the boat, arms over her head. Fergus whined, pressing himself against her, and she flung an arm around him, protectively.

Desperately, the two boys heaved on the oars, trying to slow the boat's progress. But nothing would work. The boat was speeding straight for the grate. A collision was seconds away.

Look up, little maid, the mysterious old voice said. *There are times when it is wise to wait, and times when thou must seize the moment by the tail.*

The tail? Quinn looked up and saw a rope dangling above her. It ran through a pulley to the grate. She stood up, reaching for it.

"What are you doing?" the boys called. "We're about to crash! Get down!"

Swaying precariously, Quinn ignored them. She grasped the rope and yanked it hard. With a rusty roar, the iron grate swung up and out of the way, and the boat shot out into the expanse of water. Quinn was knocked off balance and fell back into the boat, her landing softened by the cushions and blankets. The grate swung down and closed with a shudder behind them.

The boat spun and slowed and eventually came to a stop against a stone wall. Tom caught hold of an iron ring, to stop the boat from sliding away again.

"How did you know to do that, Quinn?" Sebastian wanted to know.

"I just . . . I just saw the end of the rope approaching and thought maybe it would lift the grate," Quinn lied. She was too exhausted, and too puzzled by the mysterious voice in her head, to even try and explain.

It was almost dawn. The water was now a pale gray under the swirling mist, the sky above even paler. Quinn saw a low dark archway to either side, and, beyond, the black silhouette of trees and hills and the pointed roofs of houses. She realized they had come out under the bridge. To the left was the harbor with the town of Wolfhaven crouched on its shores. To the right the river wound its way through meadows and forest, heading northeast. The tide was going out, which meant the boat was being dragged towards the harbor.

Quickly Tom tied the boat up to the ring in the stone wall, then blew out the lanterns. "We don't know if the town has been taken over by the invaders," he explained. "Until we find out, we don't want anyone to see us. All the river traffic would go under the central arch, so we're completely hidden here."

"What shall we do?" Elanor asked. Her face was white in the dim dawn light, her hazel eyes enormous.

"Let's see what's happening in the town," Quinn said, taking a telescope from the cupboard. She looked through its eyepiece at the town. It was hard to see much, the mist was so thick, but every now and again it swirled away, giving her a glimpse of the streets.

Everything was strangely peaceful. She saw a woman on her knees scrubbing her front steps. A milkmaid led her cow from door to door, a yoke with two pails set upon her shoulders. A baker was setting out fresh rolls in his window.

"It's like nothing has happened," she said, baffled.

Sebastian tried to seize the telescope from her, but she shoved him away. "Wait!"

She trained the telescope on the castle, sweeping it along the battlements. Suddenly she stiffened. A tall black form in a helmet with boar tusks stood on the castle ramparts. He was issuing orders with a forceful fist. The skeletal shapes of bog-men scuttled away, thousands of them.

"The tusked knight," she whispered. "I think he's looking for us."

"We need to get away," Tom said. "Hide out in the forest."

"Hide?" Sebastian said scornfully. "We should be rousing the town, and gathering an army."

"No, it's smart," Tom replied. "If we try to rescue anyone now, we'll only get caught ourselves. No one in the town can stand against that tusked knight and his bog-men. We'll only get them and ourselves killed. No, we need to get help first."

"Tom's right," Elanor said. "What can we do, four of us alone?"

Fergus gave a little whuff and she rubbed his ears.

"I'm sorry, Sir Fergus. Four children and one brave dog."

"We should go now, while there's still mist to hide us," said Tom. "It might burn off as the sun comes up and then we'd be seen."

"The tide's against us," Quinn said. "We'll have to row."

Everyone groaned. They were all so tired, no one really wanted to spend the next few hours rowing against the tide.

"We mustn't be caught," Elanor said. "If we are taken prisoner too, then who shall rescue my father and his people?"

"We'll just have to bend our backs to it," Sebastian answered, flexing his arm muscles.

"You'd best be quiet," Tom said. "If that's possible."

Sebastian reddened and seized one oar. "I'll go first!"

"No, I will!" Tom seized the other.

"You're both as noisy as cats in a fight," Quinn said. "*I'll* row!"

She took the oars and began to maneuver the boat

out onto the misty river. Slowly, they glided away from the bridge.

A shout rang out above them. Two knights had been standing guard on the bridge. They must have seen the shape of the boat through the mist. "Ahoy! Over here!" one shouted.

"Look, they wear my father's wolf insignia!" Elanor cried in excitement. "They can help us!" She stood up and waved at them.

The two knights suddenly lifted their bows and aimed at the boat. "Watch out!" shrieked Quinn. One arrow whizzed so close to Elanor's face, it raised a thin red welt along her cheek. She stumbled back, her hand to her face.

"But . . . they're my father's men . . ."

"Must be the invaders in disguise," Tom said, as the sound of galloping hooves disturbed the mist. "Everybody down!"

The knights began chasing them along the harbor's edge, little more than dark, racing shapes in the fog.

"Quick, let's put up the sail," Quinn cried. Then, when everyone else looked around, worried and confused, she said, "Here, Tom, take the oars and row, while I do it. We need to get away!"

Quinn lifted the mast up from where it lay in the bottom of the boat, and set it in its socket. Sebastian held it steady for her while she secured it with pins, and then together they unfurled the brown sail. Tom, meanwhile, had been gallantly rowing while Elanor kept an eye on the riders, who were drawing closer to them with each stride. The first rider released the reins as he lifted high a bow and arrow. The arrow had been set alight. "Fire!" cried Elanor, as it soared toward them, leaving a stinking trail of smoke and ashes.

A wind sprang out of nowhere, and the sail bellied out. The boat sprang forward, and the arrow fell into their wake, sizzling as it hit the water. The rider aimed another fiery arrow, but it was too late. With the wind behind them, the boat surged ahead, and the galloping riders were left far behind.

The children shouted with relief and Sebastian pumped his fist into the air.

"Good-bye," Tom called. "Hope to never see you again."

"Thank you, Owl-Eyes," Quinn said, and patted the side of the boat as if it was a dog or a horse.

"Thank you," Elanor said, her eyes shining. "Thank you, all of you."

The boat sailed on into the mist. The rocking motion lulled the exhausted children. An hour passed, and then another, and still the boat sailed on up the river. One by one, the children laid down their heads on their arms. "I'm so tired," Elanor murmured.

"Me too," Tom said, huddling the gray cloak close around him. "But we should push on. We're still too close to the castle."

But then Quinn yawned, and they all yawned with her. Even Fergus, showing a lolling pink tongue and sharp pointed teeth.

"Need . . . to . . . rest," Quinn said. She was so tired her whole body ached. She yawned again, so widely her jaw made a cracking sound, and drew her shawl closer around her.

"Maybe we can stop . . . just for a little while," Tom replied. He steered the boat towards the shore and tied it to a low-hanging branch.

"One of us should stand guard," Sebastian said, lifting his head from his arm.

"Fergus will," Tom said. Fergus's ears pricked up. "Fergus, guard," Tom added.

"Good dog," Elanor murmured.

The wolfhound's tail thumped in response.

"All right then. Just for a minute or two." Sebastian lay down again, his arm flung across his eyes.

The only sound was the *lap, lap, lap* of the river against the boat's wooden sides. Fergus yawned again and stretched out across Tom's feet. His ears slowly sunk. He shut his eyes and began to snore.

Nobody heard him. They were all fast asleep.

⟵ « ARGUING » ⟶

Elanor stirred and opened her eyes. She looked up into leafy fronds. She stared in wonderment. Where was her four-poster bed, with its velvet curtains?

Slowly her memory returned to her. The battle with the bog-men, the escape through the caverns under the castle, then the wild ride through the underground river on the boat with the eyes of an owl.

Elanor sat up. She was still in the boat. The other three were fast asleep, under blankets. Fergus lay with his head on his paws, one ear cocked. He lifted his head and gazed at her as she looked around.

The boat was now rocking gently against the bank

of a round green pool, under the shelter of a willow tree. Elanor could see little beyond its leafy fronds, but she could hear the roar of what sounded like a waterfall. She frowned in puzzlement. Where were they?

She spent little time wondering about it. A more pressing problem was bothering her. Elanor was in desperate need of a chamber pot. She realized with a sinking heart that she was going to have to crouch down behind a tree and relieve herself there. Her cheeks heated with embarrassment. What would Mistress Mauldred say about that?

Ladies do not pee behind trees!

Elanor had to smile at the thought. She wriggled out from under the blanket and did her best to climb out of the boat without waking anyone else up. It was impossible not to set the boat rocking, though. The other three all stirred and yawned and stretched, then looked at her, half in and half out of the boat.

"Where are we?"

"What are you doing?"

"Where are you going?"

The other three spoke almost simultaneously.

"I . . . I'm just . . . I don't know," said Elanor, as she made it to the shore.

"How did we get here?"

"What time is it?"

"Did we drift upstream?"

"I don't know," she answered again, crossing her legs awkwardly.

Sebastian turned to Tom. "You can't have tied us up very securely."

"But I did. I know I did."

"Perhaps the boat brought us here to safety," Quinn broke in. "Perhaps we tied up too close to the town, and perhaps the bog-men would have sniffed us out."

Everyone was silent, caught between amazement and unease.

"Well, we'd better work out where we are," Tom said and jumped out of the boat, "but first I need to pee!" He strode off behind the tree, and Elanor's face turned even hotter. She covered her ears so she didn't have to hear him.

Quinn grinned at her. "Let's find another tree."

The two girls went off in the other direction and

stood guard for each other, then washed their hands in the pool. It was set among willow trees, with steep rocky banks behind. At the far end of the valley was a waterfall that plunged in long, white ribbons down a cliff. To the north, mountains rose up, gray and forbidding under a heavy mantle of cloud. Mist lay over the trees in faint wisps, growing thicker to the south.

Quinn and Elanor met the boys back at the boat. Tom was busy getting out more food from the knapsacks. Fergus wagged his tail eagerly, and Tom tossed him a sausage.

"Don't eat it all," Quinn suggested, jumping back into the boat. "We're in the midst of the forest, we might have trouble finding more food."

"There's always food in a forest," Tom responded blithely, taking a huge bite of a pork pie.

All four children and the wolfhound busied themselves eating. No one was able to stop themselves finishing every last crumb. It must be afternoon, Elanor thought. It was hard to tell since the sun was hidden behind the fog. They must have slept the morning away.

"I've been thinking," Sebastian burst out. "Someone must have unlocked the gate to let all those black knights and those leathery bog creatures into the castle. How else could they have gotten in so easily?"

"I saw someone unlocking it," Tom said. "With the key from the great hall."

"Who was it?" Sebastian demanded.

"I didn't see their face," Tom answered. "They were wearing a hooded cloak, and it was dark."

"It had to be someone from inside the castle," Quinn said. "Else how did they get the key?"

"Oh, no, surely not," Elanor whispered.

No one liked the thought of a traitor in the castle.

"No one would," Elanor repeated. "I can't stop thinking of my father, taken prisoner, and all the castle folk too. What if they've been hurt? We have to rescue them."

"But how?" Sebastian asked.

"We have to go and find the four magical beasts," Quinn said. "Then we can wake the sleeping heroes and defeat the enemy."

"That witch of yours is wandering in her wits,"

Sebastian retorted. "There are no sleeping heroes under the castle. It's just an old story. Like dragons and unicorns. Everyone knows they don't really exist."

"But what if they do? Arwen said the world is full of magical things and we just need to have an open heart to see them."

"She also said stones could sing," Sebastian answered.

"Maybe they can," Quinn replied stoutly. "After all, who could ever imagine that Wolfhaven Castle would be stormed by men made of leather and bone?"

"We need to find help," Elanor said. "We can't rescue everyone by ourselves."

"My mam said to go and find my father," Tom said.

"So where's he?" Sebastian asked.

"In the forest somewhere," Tom answered.

"But *where* in the forest?"

Tom shrugged and looked uncomfortable. "She said to look for him where the wolves howl."

At the word "wolves," Fergus's ears pricked up and he growled softly.

Sebastian looked disgusted. "Where the wolves

howl? That's not much help. They howl everywhere."

"But the prophecy mentioned wolves," Quinn argued.

"And it also mentioned *unicorns*," Sebastian snapped back. "Besides, what good is just one man? We need an army! We should go to the nearest castle and beg the lord to help us."

"Yes," Elanor cried. She thought of being safe behind castle walls, with a soft bed to sleep in . . . and chamber pots. "Yes, let's do that."

"So where are we?" Sebastian asked.

"There was a map in the locker," Quinn said. She pulled it out and they unfolded it, four heads leaning together to examine it.

Spread out before them was the Kingdom of Stormness, guarded by mountains to the north and east, and by blue ocean to the south and west. The land was shaped like a running girl, one arm stretched before her, skirts billowing. Wolfhaven Castle was like a gemstone on the blue river and harbor that made up her choker necklace. The long chain of castles that guarded Stormness from her enemies to the east ran

down like buttons to the king's stronghold, Stormholt
Castle, the jeweled tip of her slipper, far to the south.

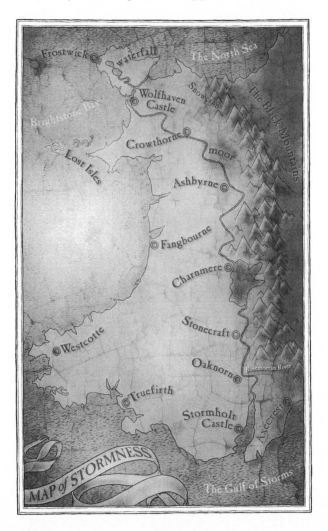

But the boat had sailed upriver, to the wild north.

"I think this must be Frostwithy Falls," Quinn replied, pointing to a picture of a waterfall far to the north. "It's the source of Wolfhaven River. That means we have traveled about six hours up the river."

"So where's the nearest castle?" Sebastian asked.

Tom put his finger on a picture of a tall, forbidding-looking castle, set on a rock in the sea, surrounded by cliffs. "It's Frostwick Castle."

"Right," Sebastian said. "That's where we'll head."

"Frostwick Castle! Lord Mortlake of Frostwick wanted to make a trade agreement with my father," Elanor said. "Surely he'll help us!"

"But the Grand Teller told us we had to wake the sleeping heroes," Quinn protested. "She didn't tell us to seek help from a lord!"

"I tell you what, if we see any sea serpents on the way, we'll grab a scale from it," Sebastian said. "In the meantime, let's try and do something practical. Getting help from someone with his own army makes a lot more sense right now."

"Still, I don't know if that's the right thing to do."

Quinn frowned. "There was something I didn't like about Lord Mortlake." Tom met her eyes, his own just as troubled. Quinn hesitated, and then pulled out the small bag of tell-stones Arwen had given her. "Let me throw the stones."

She laid out four white stones and stared at them, frowning.

"What do they say?" Tom asked.

Quinn pointed at one stone after another. "Cross-roads means it is a moment of decision . . ."

"We needed a pebble to tell us that?" Sebastian jeered.

Quinn ignored him. "Ring means that a time or a season is coming to an end, and a new one is beginning. Bird means flight, or escape, or freedom. Dark Moon means darkness and fallow times, and . . . sometimes . . . black magic."

"Well, that's reassuring," Sebastian said sarcastically.

"What does it all mean?" Elanor asked. "Surely it means that we're escaping from darkness and black magic?"

"Except the Dark Moon stone came last. That means it lies ahead of us."

Elanor gasped, then pressed her hands over her mouth. She looked imploringly at Sebastian.

He stood up. "Lady Elanor wants to seek shelter at Frostwick Castle. I think we should do what she wants. Aren't we in the employ of her father, after all?"

"Well, yes, but . . ." Tom objected.

"But nothing. What our lady desires, so I am sworn to deliver." Sebastian bowed deeply, but the boat rocked and he almost fell overboard.

Tom grinned, and Elanor tried to hide her smile. She thought Sebastian was very well mannered indeed, if rather clumsy. Mistress Mauldred would have approved of him. *A gentleman is always gallant,* she would say.

"But what if the Lord of Frostwick Castle has something to do with the invasion of Wolfhaven?" Tom interrupted. "I've been thinking . . ."

"Good heavens, a pot boy thinking," Sebastian mocked.

Tom flashed him a look of annoyance, but persevered. "I reckon it was that Jack Spry who opened the gate for the bog-men. He's the only real stranger at the castle, and it just seems all too coincidental that he should start living there only a few weeks before the castle is invaded."

"That's true," Sebastian agreed.

"No," Elanor spoke up quickly. "Jack Spry wouldn't have betrayed us. He was so grateful to us for letting him stay. He said he'd be starving in the streets if we didn't let him stay."

"A likely story," Sebastian said with disgust in his

voice. "Well, I saw him sneaking off to explore the castle. He would have seen the key hanging upon the fireplace in the great hall. He was probably checking out the best way to drag it to the gate. It's so big he couldn't lift it easily."

"I wouldn't have thought he'd be strong enough to open the gate," Quinn said.

"And I guess he was strong enough to steal all my father's silver . . ." Elanor admitted, solemnly.

"Perhaps he let down a rope for those bog-men to climb and they helped him open the gate," Tom suggested. "Anyway, Lord Mortlake brought the boy in a pie. They're in cahoots."

"Do you really think so?" Elanor asked. "Jack Spry said he hated Lord Mortlake and was glad to have been able to leave him."

"Well, he would say that, wouldn't he, if they were in cahoots." Tom looked around at the others. "Don't you see? I really don't think we should risk going to Frostwick Castle."

Elanor felt tears prickle her eyes. "But there's nowhere else for us to go. It's not safe out here in the forest. There are wolves. And bears. And witches. And bandits." She dabbed her eyes with the trailing sleeve of her dress.

"Now look what you've done," Sebastian said to Tom.

"All right," Tom said. "It's okay, Lady Elanor. We'll go to Frostwick Castle if you really think we should."

Elanor's tears dried up at once. She smiled at him radiantly.

"Just don't blame me if we all end up in a dungeon," Tom added, hoisting his knapsack onto his back.

Elanor could not help thinking that Tom could have done with a few hours reading *A Lady's Complete Guide to Manners, Morals & Modesty*. Surely a gentleman should never insist on having the last word?

FROSTWICK CASTLE

Tom left the boat tied up under the willow tree. "It may come in useful," he said. "If we need a quick escape."

Sebastian rolled his eyes. "Soon we'll be riding back to Wolfhaven Castle at the head of an army. We won't be needing a boat."

"Better safe than sorry," Tom said.

While tucking the cushions and blankets away in the locker, Quinn found a compass. "This may come in useful," she said, holding it up.

Sebastian grabbed it. "I'll take that."

"Why do you get it?" Tom said furiously, pausing in the act of tucking the map into his knapsack.

"Squires are trained to read compasses," Sebastian answered. "My guess is you've never even seen one before. I don't recall ever seeing a compass in a *kitchen*," he scoffed.

Tom went red, and jumped ashore. Without looking back, he stormed up the path, Fergus at his heels.

"You don't need to be so rude to him all the time," Quinn said, picking up the other knapsack.

"Rude?" Sebastian was astonished. "I'm not rude."

"You are," she said, and hurried up the track after Tom. Elanor followed, looking back at Sebastian with her brow all scrunched up.

Sebastian stumped along behind. He hadn't spoken with malice, he reassured himself. He was just stating an obvious truth.

The slope was steep, but there was a clear path with stone steps here and there, to make the climb easier. He soon caught up with the girls, though Tom rushed on ahead, whacking at trees with an old stick. The other three all walked in silence. Gradually they caught up to Tom, though he would not look at them.

Sebastian wondered if he should apologize, then told himself angrily that the pot boy should get over it.

The four walked on and on and on.

"There's something odd about this forest," Tom said eventually. "Have you noticed?"

"No birds," Quinn said at once.

"That's right. And no rabbits either. Or foxes. I've seen nothing living at all."

Sebastian looked around in surprise. It was true the forest was very still and quiet. "What does it mean?" He put his hand on his sword hilt. "Are we in danger?"

"I don't know," Tom replied. "Maybe it's just been hunted too much. It does mean we can't catch anything for our supper."

"I knew we shouldn't have eaten all the food," Quinn said.

After that, Sebastian kept a close eye out, but he

heard no birdsong and saw no small animals creeping through the underbrush. Tom was right. It was strange.

About an hour later, Tom stopped, holding up his hand. "I smell smoke," he whispered. "We'd best be quiet, just in case someone's ahead."

After a few more minutes, they approached a clearing where bristly-chinned men sat on fallen logs, sharpening knives and grinding the edges of sharp-looking axes. Bedrolls lay around the fire. The men were all roughly dressed, in patched breeches and cloaks of uncured hides.

Tom put his hand on Fergus's collar, keeping him quiet. Then the children dropped down to their hands and knees and crawled around the campsite, keeping their heads low and trying not to make the bracken rustle.

At last they left the camp behind them.

"Bandits, do you think?" Quinn whispered.

Tom nodded. "Nasty-looking lot. I'm glad they didn't hear us."

Sebastian wondered uneasily what his father would think. Would he approve of his son creeping through the underbrush? Sebastian did not think so. "Valor, glory, victory!" his father always cried.

Disheartened, he stamped on up the path, promising himself he would not be so chicken next time.

Eventually the path led to a narrow road which ran directly north. The trees were left behind, and they climbed through bare moorland dotted with gray rocks. A fast-running stream tumbled over rocks to the left. Mist rolled in, and then it began to rain.

They trudged on in sodden silence until they came across an old shepherd with a flock of black-faced sheep.

"Excuse me, sir," Elanor asked. "Is this the road to Frostwick Castle?"

He gaped toothlessly at her then jerked his thumb along the road. "Ahhh, urrr," he said. Elanor took that to be an affirmative.

After about another hour of walking, Sebastian saw a castle far ahead, perched on the top of a steep pinnacle of rock. He pointed it out to the other three, and they all began to walk faster, hoping to get out of the rain.

The castle seemed to play tricks with them, though, disappearing from view and then reappearing just as they began to get anxious. But it never seemed to get any closer.

The road began to rise more steeply, the land falling down sharply to a cold black lake below. Darkness closed in, and the rain fell harder.

"We should have brought the lanterns," Tom said, angry with himself for not thinking of it.

"I'm afraid." Elanor's voice trembled, glancing around the shadows.

"Don't be afraid, my lady," Sebastian said. "I'm here to protect you."

Tom snorted through his nose, but did not speak.

"It's so dark," Elanor said. "So cold, too." She rubbed her hands together and blew on them. Suddenly a small silvery light shone out from her hand. She lifted her hand in amazement, spreading her fingers. The light was shining from her moonstone ring.

"Stop!" shouted Sebastian, grabbing Elanor by the arm and hauling her back. By the light of the ring,

Sebastian had seen that they were only a step away from the edge of a cliff.

Elanor clung to his arm with both hands, white with terror, as they listened to the eerie sound of crumbling earth falling into the abyss. "Another step and I'd have gone over!"

"The Traveler's Stone," Quinn said in wonderment. "It saved you." She put her hand up to touch the wooden medallion that hung around her neck, then glanced at Sebastian's brooch.

He gave it a rub, suddenly wondering if it was more than just a cloak pin. Perhaps it had magical properties too. The thought gave him both a tingle of excitement and a shiver of fear. Sebastian did not like all these strange and marvelous happenings.

By the new light of the moonstone ring, they walked on, keeping well away from the crumbling edge of the road. All were now wet through, and stumbling with tiredness.

"Where is this blasted castle?" Tom muttered, and put his hand on Fergus's shaggy head for comfort. The wolfhound whined and shook the rain from his coat.

It glittered in the moonstone's light.

"It's sleeting," Sebastian said in disbelief. "That's not rain; it's ice."

"But it's midsummer," Elanor cried. "How can it possibly be so cold?"

"We're in the north now," Tom said.

The road began to climb steeply upward. Great boulders crouched on either side of the road, looking like hungry giants in the timid light of the moonstone ring. Without saying a word, the four children walked close together, Fergus slinking beside them.

The road wound around another bend. A light shone out ahead of them, high on the hill.

"Frostwick Castle," Elanor gasped, and broke into a staggering run.

Sebastian followed just as quickly. His calves ached, his wet boots rubbed his heels raw, and he was cold and hungry. He just wanted to get to shelter.

At last the castle appeared before them, towering high into the night sky. Only the occasional arrow slit broke the vast expanse of granite.

A narrow wooden bridge hung across a dark abyss,

leading to a huge gate. When Elanor shone the light of her moonstone ring over the edge, it showed a sharp drop down to a chasm through which the sea roiled. Sebastian led the way across the bridge, the others crowding nervously behind. Dark patches showed where slats had broken and fallen away. Water thundered far below. Sebastian put out his hand to stop the others stepping too close.

The gate loomed far above their heads, banded with iron. Elanor held up her hand, the light from her ring illuminating small sections of it. Sebastian's groping hands found a huge iron ring set into the wood. He hammered on it as loudly as he could.

Then they stood, shivering in the rain, waiting. Fergus leaned all his weight on Tom's leg. He was shivering too.

Nobody came. Sebastian hammered again.

"There's no one here," Quinn said in bitter disappointment.

"What shall we do?" asked Elanor.

"We'll need to search for some kind of shelter," Sebastian said. "A cave. Or a hut."

Everyone turned and began to cross the bridge again. The icy rain whipped their faces.

From behind came a long, slow, creaking noise. Sebastian spun in the dark, drawing his sword.

Fergus growled, and strained against Tom's hand on his collar. Elanor raised her trembling fist and shone the light of the moonstone ring into the yawning crack.

The gate was open. But there was nobody there.

Sebastian stared in astonishment, then took a few slow steps forward, his sword lifted high.

The gate opened wider.

"Is it an invitation? Shall we go in?" Elanor whispered.

"Surely it's not safe," Quinn replied.

"It's a trap," Tom said.

"Rubbish. Somebody had to open that gate. They don't just open by themselves," Sebastian answered.

"Unless it's magic," Quinn said.

The gate creaked open farther. Sebastian took a few swift steps forward, looking to see who was pushing it. He stepped back in surprise.

A little girl was standing in the gateway, holding a flickering candle in a brass candlestick. She couldn't have been much more than seven. Her long black hair looked as if it had not been combed since the day she was born. It stuck out all around her face and body in matted knots and tangles, reaching past her waist.

She was dressed in an oversized black velvet gown that fell off her thin shoulders and pooled on the ground around her. One thumb was in her mouth.

"Who are you?" Sebastian asked, squatting down to her level.

She did not answer, just stared at him with solemn black eyes.

"My name is Sebastian," he began. Suddenly he saw something move in the disheveled nest of her hair. It was a huge black rat, staring at him. Sebastian shouted and scrambled backward, falling on his backside.

The little girl smiled. She put up her free hand and stroked the rat.

"Is it some kind of pet?" Quinn asked, her voice shaking. "Is it . . . tame?"

The girl did not answer.

"We are travelers, lost in the storm," Elanor said. "We seek shelter. May we come in?"

The little girl turned and walked away, her velvet gown trailing on the ground behind her. After a few moments, the Wolfhaven four followed her.

The gate swung shut behind them, closing with a hollow boom.

THE LADY OF THE CASTLE

The guard tower was dark, silent and cobwebby. Doors swung back and forth in the wind. Leaves scuttled over the paving stones. Windows gaped with broken glass.

Tom was beginning to think the whole castle was virtually deserted when he heard the distant neighing of a horse, and the pounding of hooves on stone. He tensed, sliding his hand to his dagger. Beside him, Fergus growled. Fergus did not like this vast, cold, deserted castle any more than Tom did.

The little girl led them through the inner ward, where the neighing and the thumping of hooves were louder.

"That poor horse," Elanor said. "It'll hurt itself."

Tom looked towards the row of stables. Elanor's ring was shining brightly, showing the heavy bolts that secured one of the doors. The shrill neighing and pounding of hooves was coming from inside that stable.

"Come on," Sebastian called back over his shoulder. The little girl looked back too, her candle wavering in the gusty wind and almost blowing out. Tom and Elanor hurried to catch up. Behind them, the neighing became more shrill, the thunder of the hooves more emphatic.

"I don't like this place," Quinn said. "Why is that horse so troubled? And where is everyone?"

Ahead was another great arched doorway. The little girl opened one half of the door and led them inside the hall. It was a vast, shadowy space, with a high vaulted ceiling supported by oaken beams. A huge table ran down the center, its wooden top scarred from years of rough use. Iron candelabras hung above it, dripping icicles of wax nearly as large as those stone structures in the underground cave. Hanging on the wall were hundreds of animal skulls, many with antlers, tusks or horns.

At the far end was the grandest fireplace Tom had ever seen. It was large enough to roast a dragon, if such things existed. A small fire smoldered within, hardly big enough to roast a sparrow. It cast a faint orange light over the floor, which was carpeted with animal hides. Many hundreds of them were spread down the length of the hall, overlapping each other. Tom saw thick black bear skins, deer hides, wolf pelts, the fur of foxes, beaver, rabbits and sables, plus many more he could not identify.

"Someone likes hunting," said Sebastian.

Quinn's bare toes curled. She looked a little sick.

The wolf pelts reminded Tom of the wild man and the warning he had given. He had been right. Danger had come, and the castle had been invaded. Tom's mother and all his friends were prisoners. If only Tom had made more effort to warn the lord . . . If only he had insisted on delivering the message. Perhaps the castle could have been saved. Tom gripped his longbow and promised he would not fail in this quest.

He had to find the four magical beasts and awaken the sleeping heroes!

"I do not like this place, either," Elanor said, looking around her, timidly.

The little girl crossed the hall, leading to a door that showed steps leading up. She turned to them and beckoned, and reluctantly the four followed.

The little girl took her thumb out of her mouth so she could lift the heavy folds of her dress as she climbed the stairs. On her feet were high-heeled satin shoes, also far too big for her. Her legs were stick thin and ice white. Sebastian followed close behind, his hand on his sword hilt. Tom brought up the rear, looking around warily. On all sides were bare, empty rooms. There were no carpets or tapestries, no side tables or brass bowls, no chairs, chests or beds. Fergus's toenails clicked loudly on the stone.

Up and up they climbed, into the tower. At last the little girl opened a doorway and led the way into a room that blazed with warmth and light.

A fire blazed on the hearth. Silver candelabras filled with candles glimmered from the mantelpiece and table, and red velvet curtains shut out the sound of the wind and the rain. A chaise lounge in the same color was drawn up by the fire, and the most beautiful lady Tom had ever seen reclined upon it. Her hair and eyes were black, her skin was white, and she was dressed in a gown of red silk, embroidered with golden roses and pale lilies. Her sleeves were long and flowing, showing golden silk beneath. She wore ropes of golden pearls, and a huge ring flashed red fire on her left hand.

She stood up as the children came into the room and held out her hands. "Why, how lovely. Visitors! Welcome to Frostwick Castle. I am Lady Mortlake."

"*Lady*, my foot," muttered a low voice from the corner. "My son found you starving on a street corner. You are no more a lady than I am a maiden."

Tom craned his head and saw a skinny old woman sitting on a low stool, bent before a spinning wheel. She was dressed in what looked like a sack. A large hooked nose jutted through gray hair that straggled around her bony face. She was spinning dirty gray wool into lumpy thread.

Lady Mortlake drew herself up, her eyes flashing with fury. "How dare you? One day you will regret how you speak to me—"

She cut herself short, rearranging her face into a sweet smile. "Please don't mind my mother-in-law, she's so old she doesn't know where she is, or what she does."

"I know enough to recognize a bloodsucking leech when I see one," the old woman mumbled through stumps of teeth.

Lady Mortlake's smile stiffened. She beckoned the children towards the fire, away from the old woman at her spinning wheel. "Now, who are you, dear children, and what can I do to assist you?"

Elanor swept a graceful curtsey. "I am Lady Elanor of Wolfhaven Castle. I beg pardon for our intrusion, but we have come to ask for help and shelter."

For a moment Lady Mortlake stood motion-less, as if surprised. Then she smiled and swept forward to embrace Elanor. "My dear, sweet child. How lovely to meet you. I have heard so much about you! Heavens, you are even prettier than I had expected.

Come and sit down and let us get acquainted. For, if I am to be your new mama-in-law, we must be friends, mustn't we?"

Elanor gave a little squeak of distress. "Oh, no . . . I'm sorry, my lady, but there's some kind of misunderstanding. There is no betrothal . . . your son Cedric and I are not to be married . . . My father wants me to marry for love, as he did. But not for some time."

"I see," the lady of the castle said slowly, her hands dropping from Elanor's shoulders. She sat down again, arranging her skirts more becomingly. "Why then are you here?"

"Our castle has been attacked, and my father taken prisoner. We had to escape in the dead of the night. Oh, we have walked so far and we are so tired and hungry. Please will you help us?"

"Of course," Lady Mortlake smiled. "Are we not friends and allies?"

"How do you plan to help anyone but yourself, you greedy fool?" said the old woman malevolently. "There's not a man left in the place, nor a sword that's not as blunt as a butter knife. As for food and shelter? The barrel is empty, have you forgotten? There's not a crumb in the house, not a heel of dry bread, not a sausage."

Fergus beat his tail on the carpet and whined hopefully at the last word.

"Good heavens!" Lady Mortlake said, pressing one hand against her nose. "What on earth is that?"

"He's a dog," Tom replied shortly.

"A dog," the lady replied, her nostrils wrinkling. "How . . . how . . . *lovely*. Does he eat much? Because I'm afraid my dear, sweet mother-in-law is right. We were not expecting visitors, and our larder is rather bare . . ."

"So it has been for years, ever since you married my poor son and spent all his coin," the old woman snapped.

"Enough!" Lady Mortlake shrieked. She took a few deep breaths, then smiled again. "Please forgive my poor, dear mother-in-law. She is getting more scatterbrained every day."

"Scatterbrained! I'll have you know my wit is as sharp as a blade. So is your tongue, worst luck."

Lady Mortlake clasped her hands together. "I do hate meanness of spirit . . . it's like a dagger to my heart."

The old woman harrumphed.

There was a long, uncomfortable silence. Lady Mortlake looked up and tried to smile. "But enough about me and my problems. You said you need my help? Anything! Simply tell me what you require."

Elanor leaned forward in her eagerness. "My father's castle has been attacked. We need help . . . men and arms . . ."

"Ah, impossible. My husband and his men are away from home."

Elanor clasped her hands together. "My father and all his people have been taken prisoner. We need to rescue them!"

"But what can we do? No, it's totally impractical."

"We need to raise an army, we need to rouse the country folk and ask them for help, we need to march back to the castle—"

"March? I? Oh, my sweet girl, it's out of the question."

"But what of your husband and his men? Can we not send a message to them?"

"But who would carry the message? My poor daughter?" She indicated the little girl, big eyed and sucking her thumb. "My poor, mad mother-in-law?" She waved at the old woman. "I? It is utterly unfeasible."

"I could take a message to the lord," Sebastian said. "Just tell me where to go."

"Me too!" Tom cried.

"We'll all go," Quinn said.

Lady Mortlake tinkled an affectionate laugh. "Oh, sweet children. What kind of hostess do you think I am, to send you out into the howling storm at midnight? No, no, it simply cannot be done."

For a moment, Elanor drooped. But then she rallied herself. "If you could give us a bed for the night, we'll go in search of your husband in the morning."

"A bed? My sweet, there's not a spare stick of furniture in the place. All sold, I'm afraid."

"Except for your own four-poster," the old woman pointed out.

"Well, yes, but I can hardly be expected to be turned out of my own bed for a mob of uninvited children." Lady Mortlake shuddered. "Not to mention that beast you call a dog."

Fergus thumped his tail.

"There must be somewhere we can sleep," Quinn exclaimed.

"You can put us anywhere. Even in the stable, if you like," Elanor said.

Lady Mortlake looked horrified. "No, no, I couldn't do that."

"We are so tired," Quinn said.

"And hungry," Sebastian added.

Lady Mortlake sighed. "You want food too? Surely I've explained there's not a crumb in the whole castle."

They all stood in silence, drooping in disappointment. Nobody knew what to do.

"Eugenie! Stop sucking your thumb! Do you want teeth like a rabbit?" Lady Mortlake snapped. Eugenie took her thumb out of her mouth. Lady Mortlake waved a languid hand. "Well, it's late and I am sure you are all tired. Eugenie! Put our dear guests in the Queen's Suite."

"That doesn't sound too bad," Quinn said reassuringly to Elanor, who was looking very white and anxious.

Eugenie took the four children to a vast, echoing room with an old straw mattress tossed in a corner. The glass in the windows was broken, the hearth was filled with fallen birds' nests, and cobwebs draped the empty candelabra. Even worse, the little girl took away the only candle when she left.

Tom did not much like the look of the mattress, which was half chewed by rats, and so they huddled together in the corner of the room, hungry, cold, tired, and miserable.

"What is more powerful than love, and more evil than hatred?" Quinn said dreamily. "The poor have it and the rich need it. The dead taste it all the time, but if the living eat it, they will die."

"Whatever it is, it sounds horrible," Elanor said.

"Quinn, now's not the time for riddles." Tom spoke wearily, his head resting on his arm.

"Every time is the time for riddles."

"I don't get it," Sebastian said. "What are you talking about?"

"Yet you yourself spoke the answer," she said.

"Quinn, don't be so annoying. I wish you'd never gotten apprenticed to that stupid witch," Tom said.

"Arwen is not stupid! And riddles are not stupid either. They make us wise."

Elanor said timidly, "But how?"

Quinn spoke with deep fervor. "Riddles make us think harder and deeper and stronger. They make us look at the world aslant. They teach us that we can solve what seems unsolvable, if we try hard enough."

"So our bellies are empty and we're freezing cold. How can you solve that?" Sebastian spoke with heavy sarcasm.

Tom jumped up. "Let's go down to that great hall. We can throw some more wood on the fire, and wrap ourselves in those animal skins."

"A fine idea, except for the animal skins," Quinn said, getting up. "I am so stiff and cold. Look, my shawl is so wet I can wring water out of it!"

Sebastian pulled Elanor to her feet. "Come on. If we get a good night's sleep, it'll all seem better in the morning."

Fergus yawned, got to his feet and stretched, then followed his master with a wagging tail. Tom groped his way through the darkness to the door, then turned the door handle and pulled.

The door did not open.

He yanked harder, twisting and pulling the handle so hard the door rattled. Then he kicked it. "We've been locked in!"

16

PRISONERS

Tom was furious with himself. How could he have been so stupid? He had suspected that Lord Mortlake was somehow involved with the invasion of his home, yet he had let himself be persuaded to walk straight into a trap.

Now they were prisoners.

"We have to escape," he said.

Sebastian ran to the window, opening the casement wide and leaning out. The wind blew his red curls back. "We're too high here, we can't climb out," he called over his shoulder.

"If we had any sheets and blankets, we could have tied them together to make a rope," Quinn said.

"Fergus can't climb down a rope," Tom said. "And there's no chance I'm leaving him behind."

"Hey, someone's signaling," Sebastian said.

The other three rushed to the window, and looked out. From one of the tower windows, a light was being flashed. On and on it went, then suddenly, far away, another light flashed in response. Three times it flashed, and then both lights were blown out. "My guess is Lady Mortlake is letting her husband know he's got to come home," Tom said. "We have to get out of here before he returns!" He went back to the door and shook the handle again, then bent and looked through the keyhole. "I can't see anything. Elanor, could you get that ring of yours to shine again?"

"I don't know what I did to make that happen," she answered, coming to stand beside him. She rubbed the ring with her finger, but nothing happened. She rubbed it again. "Please light up for me," she coaxed it.

"Try blowing on it," Quinn suggested. "You blew on your hands to make them warm, do you remember?"

As soon as Elanor blew on the ring, it began to glow again. By its soft light, Tom was able to see that the key had been left in the keyhole. He thought for a moment, then went to his knapsack and got out the map. He unfolded it and slid it under the door.

"What on earth are you doing?" Sebastian said.

"I'll show you," Tom answered. He poked at the key with the tip of his dagger. The key fell out and landed with a plop on the map on the other side of the door. Tom drew the map back under the door, and the key came with it. Tom picked it up, unlocked the door, then bowed extravagantly.

"That was quite clever," Sebastian admitted.

"Why, thank you," Tom said. "Now let's get out of here."

They tiptoed out into the corridor, and Tom locked the door behind them and pocketed the key. "That'll bamboozle them."

"Good idea," Quinn said.

"Now, which way . . ." Elanor said, looking left, then right. "Does anyone remember?"

The corridor stretched a long way in either direction, bare and dusty and dark. The light from Elanor's moonstone ring only illuminated a small area.

Fergus took a few steps to the left and turned back to look at them, whining an enquiry.

"Let's go that way," Tom said.

They ran after the wolfhound, who led them through the empty echoing castle and down flight after flight of steps. It seemed to take hours, and Tom began to fear they would never find their way out.

At last, Fergus led them to the kitchen, a vast, damp place scuttling with cockroaches. Empty flour bins lay on their side, and sacks drooped sadly, spilling dust. Fergus went up to a cupboard door at the far end, and sniffed it. Then he looked back hopefully at Tom, wagging his tail.

"That cupboard's padlocked," Quinn said. "Do you think . . . ?"

"I do," Sebastian said, and drew his sword. With one strong blow he smashed the chain.

For a moment, they all froze, listening intently, but there was no cry of alarm, or any sign that anyone had heard them.

"Look!" Tom pointed. "So much for there not being a crumb to eat in the castle!"

The cupboard door had swung open and revealed fat hams hanging on hooks, rows of smoked ducks and baskets filled with dried cod. The shelves were stacked with jars of preserves. Rounds of cheese in red wax sat next to long loaves of bread sprinkled with salt and rosemary, while a plate was piled high with jam tarts.

Sebastian's eyes gleamed. "Let's grab what we can and get out of here," he said, seizing a jam tart in either hand. "Serves them right for locking us up."

"Serves them right for giving us nothing to eat," Quinn said. "Which, by the way, is the answer to my riddle."

Tom took down a ham, Quinn seized two loaves of bread, and Sebastian crammed one of the jam tarts into his mouth and grabbed a wheel of cheese. Elanor hesitated. "Oh, do you think we should?"

"We need to eat," Sebastian said through a mouthful of crumbs. "Lady Mortlake was just downright mean. The woman locked us up! Who knows what she had planned for us."

Quinn clasped both hands together at her heart, as

they'd all seen Lady Mortlake do. "*I do hate meanness of spirit . . . it's like a dagger to my heart.*"

Elanor laughed. A most unexpected dimple flashed in her cheek. Tom realized he had never seen her laugh before. "They did lock us up," she said. "I guess that means we are at war with them."

"Yes, the spoils of war," Sebastian cried.

Elanor stepped into the pantry. "Look! Everything is stamped with our insignia!"

She showed the others the wolf stamp on the wax seal on the jars. "This must have been stolen from Wolfhaven merchants. Father said the boats were being attacked by bandits!"

"Lord Mortlake's bandits, by the looks of it," Sebastian said.

"Then in that case we should take as much as we can carry," Elanor said, grabbing a sack and filling it.

"Good idea," Tom said, throwing sacks and jars into his knapsack till it bulged. Quinn and Sebastian did the same.

"Now let's go!" Elanor cried.

They hurried out of the kitchen, looking for some way out. "Where shall we go once we get out of here?" Tom panted, racing along the dark corridor.

"Listen to the storm," Quinn said. She could hear the ice hitting the windows. "We need to find shelter somewhere."

"We need to get away from here as fast as we can," said Sebastian, urgently.

"Let's head to the forest," Quinn replied. "We can take refuge under the trees."

"There's that horse in the stable," Elanor said. "We would get along much faster if we took turns riding it."

Tom looked at her in admiration. "Good idea."

"Let's go!" Sebastian urged.

THE ⇒──────→
WITCHING TIME

*B*eware, little maid. Danger comes.

Quinn peered into the darkness, her pulse jumping. "Who's there? Who spoke?"

It is the midnight hour, the witching time. Thou must beware.

"What's wrong?" Tom whispered. "Did you hear something?"

"I . . . I don't know." Quinn's hands felt for the wooden medallion that hung around her neck. It was warm, even though the air around her was so cold her breath puffed white.

She and her friends were lost in the cavernous halls of Frostwick Castle, unable to find any door or window that was unlocked and unbarred.

"There must be a way out," Elanor whispered, exhausted. The light sank as her strength diminished.

"I'll bash down the very next door we come to," Sebastian promised her. "No matter the noise I make."

Beware! The voice grew urgent.

"Let's run," Quinn urged. "Come on!"

They broke into a stumbling jog, heedless of the sound of their footsteps in the echoing darkness.

Fergus growled deep in his throat and stopped, stiff legged, all his fur bristling along his spine. Looking ahead, Quinn saw the shape of an arched doorway illuminated by a faint flicker of candlelight.

The light blossomed like a pale death lily. At its heart was a frail shadow.

The captives whirled to run, but even as panic coursed through her blood, Quinn stopped and looked back over her shoulder. She recognized the shape of the stick limbs and wild black hair of the little girl who had opened the front door to them. "Eugenie," she whispered.

The little girl approached silently, carrying her

candle before her. She was still dressed in the trailing black velvet gown, though now her feet were bare. As she came closer, Quinn saw the rat's beady eyes staring out from the tangled mass of hair. The little girl beckoned urgently, one finger held to her lips.

Fergus stopped growling, though his tail was sunk low. Quinn stood still, afraid but wondering, hearing the rapid beat of her friends' feet racing away.

A child of silence, the mysterious old voice said very softly. *Yet she hears all.*

The little girl stopped before Quinn and laid her finger on the wooden face of the necklace. Her face was grave and puzzled.

Greetings, little maid, the voice said.

The little girl bowed her head.

In great wonderment, Quinn touched her necklace. She lifted the Grand Teller's gift so she could see it. The medallion was small enough to fit into the palm of her hand. It was carved into the likeness of an old man's face, though his hair and beard were made of oak leaves. She had always thought the eyes were shut, as if the old man was sleeping, but she now saw that the eyes were open, gazing up into hers.

Beware, danger comes, spoke a voice in her mind. It was not the deep, old voice she had heard before, but a high, sweet, tremulous voice.

Quinn looked back at the little girl, and saw that her face was filled with tension. The girl gestured towards the windows, and Quinn rushed to see. Through the tiny panes of glass, she could see a group of horsemen galloping up the hill towards the castle, all carrying flaring torches of flame. In the front was the man wearing boar tusks fixed to his helmet.

I will show you the way out, the little girl said silently. *But you must be quick.*

"Tom!" Quinn called. "This way!"

Tom had stopped and turned, looking back at her in worry. She beckoned, and saw his eyes fall upon the little barefoot girl. For a moment he hesitated. "We can trust her," Quinn urged. "She'll help us."

Still he hesitated.

"The man with the boar tusks is coming!" Quinn cried in desperation. "We have to get out of here. She'll show us the way out."

Tom made a swift decision. "Elanor! Sebastian! Come this way."

The pair were both a long way down the corridor, but slowed and looked back. They saw the little girl standing in her halo of light, beckoning.

"Have you lost your minds?" Sebastian panted. "She's one of them! She locked us up!"

Fergus trotted up to the little girl and looked up at her with his wise brown eyes. She stroked his head and he wagged his tail. That decided it for Elanor, and she scurried to join them.

Sebastian groaned, flung up his hands in exasperation, and raced to follow her.

Come this way, Eugenie whispered in Quinn's mind. *But be quiet as you can. My mother is near.*

"We must be quiet," Quinn said. "Lady Mortlake is near."

Tense and silent, the four friends followed the little girl and her circle of wavering light. The click of Fergus's nails on the stone seemed very loud.

Eugenie led them through the maze of galleries and staircases, till they reached the great hall. Its vaulted ceiling was hidden in shadows. Skulls of long-dead animals leered down at them. The embers of the fire were a cluster of small blinking red eyes. Eugenie then led them to a small side door and drew a key from her pocket. In a moment, the door was unlocked and they were thrust into the tumult of the storm. Icy rain lashed Quinn's face. A taloned wind yanked at her hair. It was so cold, the bones of her face ached.

As they hurried down into the inner ward, Quinn saw that the gateway was open. She could hear the thunder of the horses' hooves, and she could see the red glare of the riders' torches. The knights galloped up the hill and across the wooden bridge. In seconds they would be upon them.

"Hide!" Sebastian cried, looking all around him.

Eugenie beckoned them, and again they had no choice but to follow her. She led them, stumbling in the blinding wind, towards the stable. Beside the double doors were a row of barrels. The five children and the dog crouched down behind them, Tom's hand on Fergus's muzzle to keep him quiet.

The horses came to a rearing, snorting stop in the middle of the courtyard. The knights dismounted heavily, their armor clanking. The acrid smoke from their torches stung Quinn's eyes. She crouched lower, hoping desperately not to be seen.

A troop of bog-men came loping through the gate, their bony legs working tirelessly. The man in the tusked helmet pointed to a far corner of the courtyard. "Wait there," he ordered.

The bog-men silently obeyed, standing in orderly ranks. The torchlight flickered over their hideous faces, highlighting the taut, blackened skin, the eyeless sockets and twisted mouths. The air was filled with the stink of rotting eggs.

"You deign to answer my summons, at last!" Lady Mortlake shrieked, striding down the steps of the castle, her black hair whipping behind her.

The man with the boar tusks took off his helmet. Quinn bit back a gasp.

It was Lord Mortlake.

"Why did you signal me? I have much to do if I'm to keep Lord Wolfgang and his people crushed under my heel." Lord Mortlake slapped his gauntlets into his hand, looking thunderously angry.

"What took you so long?" his wife screeched. "I have news, important news."

"We galloped the whole way, almost rode the horses into the ground," said Lord Mortlake. He gestured towards the sweat-lathered horses, standing with hanging heads and heaving sides. "You'd better have a good reason for dragging us all this way."

"Lord Wolfgang's brat is here!" she cried. "She came looking for *help*!"

Lord Mortlake strode forward and gripped her wrist with one hand. "Lady Elanor? Here?" He looked around, his eyes fierce as an eagle bending to its prey. "Where?"

"Luckily for you, I locked the brat up," Lady Mortlake answered. "Let me go, you're hurting me."

Lord Mortlake shook her roughly. "Where is she? I must have her. As long as she's free, she's a risk to me."

"Don't you worry, I have her safe," Lady Mortlake sneered. She jerked her hand and at last he let her go, frowning down at the cobblestones.

"To keep her or kill her?" he mused out loud.

Elanor turned big, anxious eyes towards Quinn, who squeezed her hand in comfort and pressed her finger to her lips.

"*Kill* her!" Lady Mortlake ordered.

He held up a hand to silence her. As he thought, she paced to and fro, gnawing at her full red lips.

"Perhaps killing her would be best," he said at last. "I want no complications."

He was answered with a rush of color to his wife's face and a radiant smile. She swept up to him, clasping his arm with both hands as she reached up to kiss his unshaven cheek. "I think that's best," she said, sweet and low. "You are so wise."

The knights unsaddled the horses and led them into one of the stables. Some of the horses were so exhausted they could scarcely stumble along. One had a thin figure draped over the saddle. In the light of the torches thrust into brackets on the stable wall, Quinn recognized the lank, dark hair of Lord Mortlake's son. "Is that Cedric?" Lady Mortlake asked. "What's wrong with him?"

"He passed out a while back," Lord Mortlake said.

"Such a weakling," said Lady Mortlake. "I suppose he fainted at the sight of blood. Well, at least you managed to take Wolfhaven Castle," she added. "Your plan worked."

He frowned. "Of course my plan worked. It was flawless. At least, it was until Lady Elanor slipped my leash, but we have her now."

Lady Mortlake was radiant. "And soon she'll be dead, and her stubborn father with her."

"No, I have a need of him first."

She frowned, and he tapped her under the chin.

"Never you fear," said Lord Mortlake. "He won't be alive long."

Lady Mortlake smiled and clapped her hands together.

Lord Mortlake looked up at the castle. "So where is she?"

"I'll take you to her. I warn you, she has other brats with her. And some kind of awful hairy creature."

"They will all need to die," Lord Mortlake said.

"Before we kill them, will you do something for

me? Will you kill that beast in the stable? It's been making such a racket, it has given me a headache."

"Ailith, I've fought all day and ridden all night—"

"You *want* me to have a headache? Maybe your horrible mother is trying to poison me . . . I want the unicorn's horn too."

An electric thrill ran over the children crouched behind the barrels. Quinn's and Tom's eyes met in wild excitement.

"Did she just say *unicorn?*" Sebastian whispered.

Elanor nodded, her eyes round with amazement.

"Mother's not poisoning you, Ailith," Lord Mortlake said impatiently.

His wife shouted, "If a unicorn's horn can save you from plague, pestilence and poison, it's bound to help cure a headache. Kill the wretched beast! I want the unicorn's horn and I want it now!"

"Very well," he answered, shrugging wearily.

Lady Mortlake smiled at him. "See you back upstairs." She sashayed away, and Lord Mortlake drew his sword with a swift hiss. The bog-men jerked to attention, but he waved his hand in dismissal and they relaxed back into a standing position, eye sockets staring sightlessly forward.

Lord Mortlake strode to the stables, his sword in his hand. Quinn heard the stable door being unlocked and unbolted.

A high, shrill neigh of defiance pierced the air, and Elanor's whole body tensed.

"That's enough of that," Lord Mortlake said. "I need your horn, beast."

Elanor leapt to her feet and hurtled out from behind the barrels.

"Elanor, no!" Tom cried, but she was gone.

18

←«SWORD MET SWORD»→

Tom ran after her, Quinn and Sebastian close behind.

They were just in time to see Elanor head butt Lord Mortlake from behind. "You're not killing that unicorn!" she shouted.

Lord Mortlake stumbled forward, but he was a tall, strong man and Elanor was only slight. He did not fall, but recovered his balance and spun around, his sword instantly swinging out.

It met Sebastian's sword with a clash of metal. Sebastian staggered at the force of the blow, but fought back manfully. Sword met sword, but it was an unequal contest. Lord Mortlake had immense strength, and tall as he was, Sebastian only came up to his shoulder.

"Get him, Sebastian!" Tom shouted. "Watch out!"

Sebastian was being forced back against a great pile of hay. His arm was tiring, his sword waving wildly. Tom lifted his bow and fired an arrow at Lord Mortlake. It clinked against his armor and fell to the floor. Lord Mortlake did not even look around. Instead he raised his sword and brought it down towards Sebastian in a great, sweeping arc.

Then Fergus streaked past and leapt upon Lord Mortlake, bearing him down to the ground. His great sword clattered on the cobblestones. Lord Mortlake threw the dog off him and rolled, reaching to recover his sword. Tom kicked out and sent the sword spinning away. Lord Mortlake aimed a blow as he staggered to his feet, but Tom dodged it and managed a quick kick at the back of the knight's knee. Lord Mortlake dropped to his other knee, but reached out his arm and took Tom down with him.

Sebastian rushed forward, his sword dropping unheeded as he sought to drag Tom free. Quinn seized Lord Mortlake's arm, clinging to it with all her strength. He flailed his arm wildly, and she was shaken up and down, but did not let go. Fergus, barking madly, lunged forward and clamped his teeth onto Lord Mortlake's backside, where there was a gap in his armor. Shocked, Lord Mortlake dropped Tom, spinning and trying in vain to dislodge the wolfhound.

Suddenly Elanor brought a metal bucket down hard on Lord Mortlake's head. His eyes rolled up, and he fell with a great clatter to the ground.

Panting, the four children stood around him, watching him warily. He did not move. Behind them came a soft whicker. All four pairs of eyes flew up.

It was hard to see the unicorn in the shadowy stable. Tom could only tell that the unicorn was huge, bigger even than the cart horses that pulled the farm plows. Elanor breathed on her ring, and soft light shone out, glinting on the chains that kept the great beast harnessed and hobbled. They all stared in wonder.

The unicorn's coat was the dark silvery brown of

a winter moor, his mane and tail black as night. He dipped his head and pawed the ground. A long, black, spiraling horn sprang from between his dark eyes.

"Oh, he's incredible," Elanor breathed. She ran across the stable, and began unbuckling the unicorn's hobbles. His hooves were as big as plates and fringed with shaggy black hair. He bent his head and nuzzled Elanor, as if in thanks. Fergus whined and lifted his nose, and the unicorn touched it with his black muzzle.

"Quickly!" urged Tom. "We have to get out of here!"

The beast was so tall that it was hard to reach the buckles which kept the heavy harness strapped around his back and shoulders. Sebastian had to drag over a bale of straw to stand on while he undid the straps. Quinn rushed to unfasten all the other buckles, while Tom unchained the unicorn from the wall. The unicorn had a dark stripe that ran down his spine, and more dark marks on his legs, like the streaks on the silver bark of a birch tree.

"Leave the bridle on so we can ride him," Elanor said. Her face was lit up with awe. "He's so big; he can easily carry two of us."

"Let's get away as fast as we can," Tom said. "Girls, you ride the unicorn. We'll run along beside."

"I can't ride," Quinn said, looking up at the great horned beast in trepidation.

"I can," Elanor said. She jumped up onto the bale of straw, then deftly sprang up onto the unicorn's back, tucking her skirts around her legs. "Quick, you can hang on to me." She gathered the reins as Quinn scrambled up.

Sebastian retrieved his sword and Tom's lost arrow, and the two boys ran after the unicorn. The little girl Eugenie stood next to the barrels, her thumb in her mouth.

"Thank you for helping us, Eugenie," Quinn called to her.

She nodded her head in response.

A shout of warning rang out. Tom spun around. Men were running out of the guardroom at the far end of the courtyard, wielding weapons. "Stop them!" a woman's voice shouted. "I want them captured and destroyed!"

Lady Mortlake stood on the steps, her hair flying in the wind like a tattered black mantle. Her eyes were strange and wild. The knights ran forward, swords glinting, their faces hidden behind their visors, and the bog-men came horribly to life, breaking into a run and shaking their spears.

The unicorn galloped across the courtyard, the two girls clinging to his back. Tom and Sebastian raced after them, Fergus at their heels, and the pursuing bog-men dangerously close. Then Eugenie pushed over one of the barrels, right in the path of the creatures. The barrel fell and broke, releasing a gush of some black, stinking liquid. Eugenie looked at Tom, her eyes filled with urgency, then she turned and ran into the stable.

The smell triggered a flash of memory for Tom. As he ran through the gateway, he grabbed one of the torches from its bracket on the wall and flung it behind him. At once, a great roaring wall of flame flared up. The soldiers and bog-men nearby were blown off their feet and had to scramble away to avoid being burned to death. As the flames filled the gateway, the soldiers ran for water, while Lady Mortlake screamed in anger,

"Get them! Get them!"

But flames roared between the soldiers and the escaping children.

Tom ran after his friends into the dark, stormy night. Fergus barked victoriously, bounding along at the unicorn's side. Above him, Elanor's ring blazed, lighting the way.

Sebastian looked back at Tom, grinning. "A unicorn! Who would believe it? Maybe this mad quest is not so impossible after all!"

Behind the barrier of flame, Lady Mortlake screamed. "I will find you! I will find you wherever you hide, and I'll have your guts for garters!"